# REUBEN

## AND THE AMAZING
## MIND MACHINE

JONATHAN M HUGHES

Matador
9 Priory Business Park,
Wistow Road, Kibworth Beauchamp,
Leicestershire. LE8 0RX
Tel: 0116 279 2299
Email: books@troubador.co.uk
Web: www.troubador.co.uk/matador
Twitter: @matadorbooks

ISBN 978 1800462 113

British Library Cataloguing in Publication Data.
A catalogue record for this book is available from the British Library.

Printed and bound in Great Britain by 4edge Limited
Typeset in 12pt Minion Pro by Troubador Publishing Ltd, Leicester, UK

Matador is an imprint of Troubador Publishing Ltd

To my late father-in-law Cyril F. Graysmark MSc
and his grandson Reuben,
who were the inspiration for this book.

# Chapter One

## Grandpa's Brilliant Invention

"Hey Simon, I've got something brilliant to tell you," said Reuben, his mobile phone pressed up against his ear as he walked up his grandfather's garden path.

Reuben knocked hard on the rotten front door. "My Grandfather has been developing a mind-changing machine," he continued. "And he's going to try it out today."

As he listened to Simon's reply, he looked around at the garden. Self-seeded holly hocks far too close to the house, bowed down to him in the breeze. A tomato plant growing up between two paving slabs seemed to be surviving with bright red tomatoes hanging down. The lawn was now a meadow and a butler sink half hidden under a hedge was filled almost to the top with water and brown leaves. He felt guilty that he had never offered to help his Grandfather tidy the garden, but then he'd never been asked.

The door creaked open. "Hello Reuben, come in!" said his Grandfather, a retired Professor of neuroscience. "You're a bit early, but come in my boy and we'll soon have my machine up and running."

"I've got to go Simon. I'll ring you later to let you know what happens and if it works, bye."

"Oi! I told you not to tell anyone about the Mind Machine!" scolded Gramps.

Gramps was very tall and slim with chiselled features. His white bushy hair seemed to have a life of its own, always sticking up like three wayward horns. "To be honest," continued Gramps, "you miss school too much to be any good at anything. I know your Aunt writes you a sick note anytime you want, but it's a bad habit to get into. Anyway, you know that's what I think."

"I'm not bothered about school qualifications, I want to be a rock star."

"Have you joined a rock band yet?"

"No, not yet."

"Have you started learning the guitar?"

"Well no, but I did have a couple of lessons last year."

"Dreaming is a curse to you youngsters today," said Gramps. "You have to make things happen. Anyway, I think you should work hard at school *and* be in a rock band. You shouldn't put all your eggs in one basket. At fourteen, you probably only have two more years at school, you should make the most of it. "

"Yeah, I suppose so," said Reuben, pleased that Gramps hadn't totally dismissed his rock star ambitions. He then followed Gramps into the musty-smelling hall. A sagging net curtain hung down over a small window. The dark red carpet looked even more threadbare than he remembered from only a few days ago. Reuben squinted his eyes to be able to see his reflection in the large dusty mirror. He ran his fingers through his long blonde fringe. While still staring at himself in the mirror, he opened his mouth slightly and bit his teeth together, in a wide overdone grin.

"Not staring at yourself again!" moaned Gramps. "The trouble with you youngsters, is that you think far too much about your appearance."

The cellar door creaked open and they walked down the rickety steps to the cellar, where Gramps had his workshop.

A cobweb-covered strip-light flickered into life, lighting up the workbench which was crammed with so much stuff; test tubes, coils of wire, circuit boards among many other items. Crooked shelves lined the walls and were crammed with even more clutter and old boxes with thick handwriting scrawled all over them. Gramps had spent the last fifteen years, since retiring, designing and building the electronic thought-changing machine as a project to keep himself busy.

"Actually the battery needs a bit of a charge. Come back this afternoon and it should be oven ready to go!"

"Not another delay!" moaned Reuben.

### Back at home

Reuben sat on the sagging sofa and stared at the TV while eating a slice of his Aunt's home-made quiche. A pair of hands were potting up some plants, making Reuben yawn with boredom. He looked round at the large fish tank to see Reddy and Goldy both staring at him, opening and closing their mouths, waiting for some fish flakes.

Orange curtains and the nineteen-seventies furniture made Reuben feel he was living in a scruffy museum.

"What are you going to do this afternoon?" asked his Aunt Audrey, pulling a brush through her frizzy, dyed blonde hair, then staring at the clogged bristles and yanking out some hair.

"I'm going to Gramps'. He's going to try out an electronic mind-controlling machine he's been working on."

"Oh not the thing he's been working on for over fifteen years... what a waste of time, money and effort, and of course it won't work. You'd think he would have known better. Anyway what about school today?" she said, throwing a bunch of dried hair on to the carpet.

"You wrote me another sick note, remember?"

"What illness was it this time?"

"Er, well I don't know, you wrote it down, I think it was a bit of an aching neck and a headache" said Reuben, rather irritated at her questioning.

"I'm only thinking about your well-being!" she said. "If your parents were still alive they would be horrified."

"Anyway, I'm off to Gramps' now, Auntie," he said, rising to his feet and walking over and pecking her on the cheek like he always had since a small boy. Deep down he was grateful to his aunt Audrey for giving him a home. Even though only aged five, he could still remember the horror of a policewomen trying to explain to him that his parents were dead.

# Chapter Two

## Will it Work?

"*B*last!" muttered Reuben as a large stinging nettle stung the back of his hand as he walked up the garden path towards Gramps' front door. He used the large door-knocker again as the bell hadn't worked for years. A large spider was weaving a web around a poor unsuspecting fly. Being petrified of big hairy spiders, Reuben moved back a step. He waited for what seemed like ages, then lifted the door-knocker and banged it down again. He felt pleased when the struggling fly escaped from the spider's web, then a Cabbage White butterfly flew straight into the web. Reuben just managed to put his terror of spiders to one side and offered his hand up and coaxed the struggling butterfly out of harm's way and it fluttered off to live another day.

Gramps had always been there for him, taking him out for trips and always finding time to listen.

Granny was only a distant memory. She had died instantly while crossing Ardingly High Street, apparently hit by a yob on a moped, showing off to his mates.

"Oh, hullo again Reuben," said Gramps. "I hope you haven't been waiting here long?"

"Only about five minutes."

Gramps wheezed as he lifted the machine from the cluttered kitchen table. It was about the size of a shoe box. A keyboard from an old fashioned typewriter sat sideways along the top. This was used to type in messages which could be sent, via customized microwaves, into people's minds. At the side of the machine were two small remote control levers used for controlling people's limb movements. Many switches were randomly positioned along the top and sides. Also on top sat an old riflescope to enable accurate aiming.

"Bring the tube as well," he said to Reuben.

"What tube? er which one?"

"That one over there."

Reuben suddenly felt panicky, his mind going blank, just like he sometimes felt at school when he was worried about not being able to find something, or know what to do. But he knew Gramps wouldn't get angry, unlike his teacher, Mr. Horns. He soon found the quarter meter long metal tube lying by the kettle. He walked along the hall and up the creaking stairs behind Gramps.

"This is the huge moment I've been waiting for," said Gramps, screwing the tube into the front of the machine. "Higgins doesn't realise that he will be the first 'guinea pig' trial for my new Mind-Changing Machine! Ha, ha, ha."

They both stared down from the upstairs window at Gramps' neighbour, Mr. Higgins, sitting there very relaxed in his garden chair. Clouds of smoke billowed up in the early afternoon sun light, as he puffed away on his pipe while staring at a Daily Telegraph.

"I doubt if it will really work," said Reuben.

"What?" gasped Gramps, turning round and giving Reuben a disapproving stare. "What do I keep telling you about positive and optimistic thinking? That's half your problem. You think nothing will work! You don't know or take an opportunity when it arises." He then turned back round again. "Stone the crows, he's gone in," he muttered.

"It's alright, he's walking back over to his chair," said Reuben, feeling unexpectedly excited.

Gramps' moth-eaten jacket sleeves rested on the rotting window sill as he held the machine as steadily as possible. He squinted as he peered through the sight, carefully lining up the cross-hairs with Mr. Higgins' head. He was now puffing so steadily on his pipe, clouds of smoke billowed up like a puffing steam train.

"If your machine works, it'll be fantastic!" said Reuben.

"Stop saying *if* it works!" scolded Gramps, turning round again. "AAAAGH!" he then shouted, trying to grab the machine, which suddenly started slipping out of the window. It did a complete flip through the air and crashed into an overgrown elder bush. A protesting blackbird flew for its life.

"Now it *won't* work!" Gramps blasted. "Fifteen years of working and thousands of hours all gone… ruined. I've just gone back to day one of fifteen years ago!"

"Benson seems to have thrown something out of the window," remarked Mrs. Higgins, staring up from their garden next door, at Gramp's open window.

"He might as well. His garden's a tip, an utter disgrace," said Mr. Higgins, briefly looking up from his Daily Telegraph.

Reuben followed his grandfather down the stairs and out into the weed-ridden garden, and watched in trepidation, as Gramps slowly grabbed the upright tube and pulled the machine from inside the elder bush. "It looks alright. Let's hope the bush cushioned its fall," Gramps muttered. He started frantically tapping some buttons. "Phew, it's come on and seems to be working, but please, just stop distracting me and let me get on with it!"

They walked back up the stairs.

He started tapping a few buttons again, then stared at a small dial. "It seems ready. I'm pretty sure it's alright, but there's now a scratch down one side, it took me ages to spray and polish it." He then carefully lifted it back on to the window sill and bent his head down and squinted his left eye while staring with his wide open right eye, through the sight.

Reuben continued staring down from the upstairs window at Mr. Higgins. His pale legs looked like chicken legs sticking out of a pair of brown baggy shorts. His blue short-sleeved shirt was very neatly pressed. Beautifully manicured flower beds and a super-short very green lawn looked so incongruous next door to the wilderness of Gramps' garden.

"Oi! where are my tea and buns?" Mr. Higgins shouted to his wife, without even bothering to look up at her.

"They're coming dearest!" she called out from the open kitchen window.

"Why does she call him dearest when he's so horrible?" asked Reuben.

"Well, it's a habit of a lifetime. She probably doesn't realise how ghastly he's become over the years. I bet he didn't treat her like that on their first date, many years ago."

"Hurry up then!" shouted Mr. Higgins. "Oh, I suppose I might as well go to the toilet first," he growled, slowly pushing himself up from the garden chair.

"I think this is a good time to take a break," said Gramps. "He's moving about too much now, let's have breakfast."

"Oh, what?" said Reuben. "You've taken fifteen years to build this potentially amazing Mind Machine and now you want to have breakfast first! Surely you can zap slow moving targets! Are you sure that it isn't because you just can't face the fact that it's not going to work?"

"NO…I'm hungry! I haven't eaten yet, that's why!" said Gramps angrily. "Why are you suddenly so moody, Reuben? It's not like you. Sometimes you forget how old I am."

"How could I forget? Sorry, it's just that, although it's Friday, I'm already dreading school on Monday. I'll see if Aunt Audrey will write me another sick note."

"You know, as I keep telling you, you shouldn't keep missing school unless you are genuinely ill," said Gramps. "In my day, we had it so hard compared to you youngsters."

"I've got so far behind at school now, it's almost impossible for me to catch up," groaned Reuben.

"It's a good job your dad isn't alive – he'd really have something to say about it," said Gramps.

Reuben followed Gramps into the musty-smelling kitchen. He felt his shoe soles sticking to the black and white lino floor. Biscuit tins that had been empty for years were strewn around the shelves. The cooker looked as if it hadn't been cleaned for decades. A washing machine stood at one end, its small circular door open, with old shirts, tired looking underpants and socks hanging out. Gramps tugged on a battered looking kitchen drawer, and it squeaked and groaned as it slid out. It was packed with old dull cutlery. He pulled out a stained slightly bent spoon.

"I've already tried out this electronic machine to send the brain waves to wood lice and change their behaviour," said Gramps "If I slowly move the joy stick to the left, impulses make them turn left. The same thing happens when I move the joystick to the right. All my hard work is coming to fruition! Earlier this morning, a dog came into the garden and I sent thought waves telling it to turn round and leave the garden, and it did! With an animal it must send an instinctive feeling."

"It must have been some sort of a coincidence," scoffed Reuben, pulling out an old pine chair and sitting down. "Maybe the dog could hear the owner calling it, or it suddenly felt hungry. Their hearing is way superior to ours." He then pulled out his mobile and started flicking through for messages.

"Will you put that ghastly mobile telephone away!" snapped Gramps. "You know how much I hate them."

"Sorry," said Reuben, pushing it back into his pocket. "Do you realise, if your machine is a success you'll be a billionaire overnight? Think what it could be used for!"

"Is money all you think about?" snapped Gramps. "You are so selfish sometimes Reuben. Anyway, why do I need the money? I'm old and I can't take it with me."

"I have a great idea ," said Reuben. "Why don't I try the machine on you?"

"What? I don't want those thought waves entering MY brain!" said Gramps.

"That doesn't surprise me," said Reuben, glancing at himself in a grubby mirror on the table and re-adjusting his hair with his fingers. Reuben felt that Gramps was more of a mate than a Grandfather, despite his age of eighty, but he just wished he would stop moaning.

Gramps slowly lifted the tea pot and the over-stewed tea sloshed out of the spout into the cups.

They quickly ate some slices of toast and marmalade.

"Right, shall we make a start then?" said Gramps, looking at the ceiling while gulping back his last inch of tea.

"I'm still confused by how it will work," moaned a doubting Reuben.

"You can borrow volumes three and four of 'The Elementary Electrical Impulses of Brain Matter Connections' by Professor William Bore, if you like. That might make things a bit clearer."

"No thanks," murmured Reuben. "I'm reading a story about a rescued mouse at the moment. Thanks anyway."

They walked upstairs to the open landing window and peered down at Mr. Higgins, who fortunately was still sitting on his garden chair. "Oi!" he suddenly shouted, looking up from his Daily Telegraph. "Where are my cakes?"

"Who's he shouting at now?" asked Reuben.

"His wife of course, who else?" replied Gramps. "Since he's retired, her whole life is dominated by running about after him. Anyway, let's stop wasting time talking about his selfish goings on and get on with trying out my machine. That's all I care about, not him. Hmmmm…what shall I make him say or do then? As you're my favourite grandson, I'll let you decide."

"I'm your only grandson, Anyway…er… make him say…er." Reuben leaned over and tapped his fingers on the old typewriter keys, finding it difficult to type accurately on them.

Gramps then lifted the machine, pointing it at Mr. Higgins and pushed the action button. A very loud posh lady's voice burst forth from the machine, echoing around the neighbourhood, making Reuben jump.

"GOOD MORNING. THE MESSAGE HAS BEEN SENT AND IS NOW ENTERING THE BRAIN OF A HOMO SAPIEN: THE RANGE IS APPROXIMATELY THIRTY METERS, THANK YOU."

"What on earth is all that about?" shouted Mr. Higgins, throwing down his paper and rising angrily to his feet.

"I've no idea," said Mrs. Higgins, putting down her cup of tea and Woman's Weekly, as she looked up towards the Professor's window.

"I'm sure he's gone mad," growled Mr. Higgins. "And…ak yuk sucker…ragabumplingtucker."

"Pardon dear?" replied a shocked Mrs. Higgins. "Shall I call an ambulance?"

"Don't be ridiculous. There is absolutely nothing wrong with me!"

"There MUST be something wrong with you," snapped Mrs. Higgins. "And you looked so vague and pale, when you were talking that absolute rubbish."

"Good gracious me!" gasped Gramps. "This thing is working beautifully! I can get messages sent and interwoven into normal conversation in less than a second but your spelling leaves much to be desired, Reuben."

"I find typing on those heavy stiff old keys difficult."

"I'll show you how it's done!" said Gramps, slowly typing in a message. He lifted up the heavy machine and carefully aimed it toward Mr. Higgins again.

"I've just seen some weeds!" retorted Mr. Higgins, rising to his feet and pointing to a small vegetable patch, in the middle of which stood a tatty scarecrow. "I think you should just get on with weeding!" he continued. Then his mouth fell partially open and he went very pale with vague-looking eyes, and opened his mouth wide. "Kumby yah my Lord, Kumby yah!"

he sang at the top of his voice. His mouth snapped shut and he sat back down on to his chair.

"Did you make him sing that?" gasped Reuben.

"Yes! this is INCREDIBLE I've never been so happy in all my life."

"Yes!" agreed Reuben. "It's amazing. I just can't believe it. Can I borrow it?"

"No!"

"By the way, what did that woman's voice mean by a Homo Sapien?"

"It means 'modern human regarded as a species'. Don't you learn anything at school? Sorry I forgot, you're never there, are you?"

Mr. Higgins continued sitting in his garden reading his Daily Telegraph. His watery eyes scanned the pages. "Oi! I said where are my cakes?" he bellowed again.

"Goodness me!" gasped Gramps. "He's getting worse. I feel so sorry for Mrs Higgins, she seems such a lovely lady."

"I'm coming dearest! I'm coming dearest!" Mrs Higgins called out as she staggered along the neat lawn, carrying a tray of tea and cakes. She placed the tray beside him on the garden table. She was wearing an apron and her grey hair was scraped up into a bun. "You still have a great singing voice dear."

"Pardon? I haven't sung for years!"

Without saying thank you, he suddenly leaned forward and grabbed a cake and started to rip into it, chewing wildly, as he continued staring over his half spectacles at the Daily Telegraph. He suddenly stopped chewing and looked up at Gramps' open window. "Being nosy again Benson?" he shouted. "It's a pity you don't have anything more important to do than push your ugly nose into other people's business."

"How dare you talk to me like that!" shouted back Gramps. "I've had a very responsible position as a Professor at a top university. Show more respect! I'm not interested in what you are doing. And I'm always busy doing important things."

"Shall we shut the window, and try the machine on someone else?" said Reuben. "He's starting to get really nasty."

"He's always so rude to me and now he's going to be dealt with!" said Gramps, picking up the machine. He immediately started tapping furiously on the old typewriter keys.

"What's that you're tapping into the machine?"

"You'll find out in a minute if it works the way it should."

Reuben watched with unbelieving trepidation.

Gramps crouched down again and stared through the scope. His slightly quivering pale finger pressed the action trigger again.

Mr. Higgins suddenly stopped chewing and looked pale and vague again, his glazed watery eyes were just staring ahead. The Daily Telegraph slipped off his lap and a piece of cake fell from his open mouth. He then slowly pushed himself up from his chair and stood bolt upright.

"I am a bully," he announced with a sound of great authority to his wife. "I have no respect for you and treat you like a slave. You come and sit here, love, and I'll do everything. I was born to do house work!"

"I say!" gasped Gramps. "What he said is exactly what I typed into the machine."

"Are you alright dearest?" asked Mrs Higgins, looking shocked and anxious at this sudden change in her husband's behaviour. "You could start with the dishes, then a good hoover through, and the kitchen floor could do with a good clean."

"What are you on about?" he said, sitting back down in his chair.

"Wow!" remarked Reuben.

Just at that moment, a frail old neighbour wobbled slightly as he walked into Mr. and Mrs. Higgins' garden. He was stooped over so much that his tatty tweed jacket was hanging down to his knees. His old trilby hat looked greasy and worn. His face looked like a pale wrinkled prune and he had a small bag in his hand.

"It's old Mr. Pepperdean," said Reuben. "I wonder what he's doing visiting Mr. Higgins. Let's watch and find out."

"Hullo Mr. Higgins," said Mr. Pepperdean in a frail shaky voice with a strong country accent. "I have too many organic radishes from my allotment. I was wondering whether you would, er, like a few?"

"Oh, yes I would actually," said Mr. Higgins, looking up from his garden chair and just managing a crinkled up smile, showing a few discoloured teeth. "I might order a salad from the woman tonight."

"Who?"

"The woman! You know, my wife!"

"Oh!" said Mr. Pepperdean. "Anyway, would you be happy to pay fifty-three pence for this bag of radishes?"

"I thought you were going to give them to me as a kind neighbourly gesture."

"I can't afford to give them away. I need to recoup my costs like the seeds, fertilizer, slug pellets, wear and tear on my shoe rubber while walking about getting all this stuff. The three pence on top of the fifty pence is my profit."

"I'll pay fifty pence," said Mr. Higgins, pulling a fifty pence piece from his huge fat wallet.

"No! the price is fifty-three pence!" spluttered Mr. Pepperdean, desperately trying to stick up for himself to this pompous barrister. "I told you, I can't sell them just to break even, I need the profit to live off. "

"Fair enough," growled Mr. Higgins, returning the fifty pence piece to his fat wallet. "Now get out of my garden and take the stupid radishes with you!"

"I think Mr. Pepperdean is trying to sell him a bag of radishes," said Reuben. "He knocked on our door only a few days ago. He said he makes three pence on every bag he sells. I have a brilliant idea," he suggested. "You can make Mr. Pepperdean *give* the radishes to Mr. Higgins to try to spread a bit of goodwill and kindness around the village."

"Oh, that's not what I had in mind," muttered Gramps, squinting through the scope, adjusting the focus. "And what about Mr. Pepperdean's profit?"

The garden chair fell over as Mr. Higgins suddenly rose to his feet. His face looked like that of a dead man, and his mouth fell partially open. He showed his teeth, snarling like a wolf.

Mr. Pepperdean looked rather surprised as Mr. Higgins slowly walked up to the scarecrow and grabbed it by the throat. "Oi! I told you, Pepperdean, to get out of my garden!" he bellowed right into the scarecrow's face.

Mrs. Higgins gasped, her mouth wide open. "I don't wish to concern you, Mr. Pepperdean," she said, "but I think he might think the scarecrow is you. Something's really the matter with him today. If I were you I'd leave now."

"Something's gone wrong!" gasped Gramps. "Everything's gone out of sync. He thinks the scarecrow is Mr. Pepperdean. I am a bit concerned about this. Professor William Bore did warn of this in volume three."

"This is terrible to watch!" gasped Reuben. "Can't you switch it off. He might start on Mr. Pepperdean, or worse still come over here and attack us!"

"I have hit the cancel button, but there's a slight problem…It isn't working. But not to worry, the extra brain waves will dissolve away in a minute or two. I feel really excited and worried at the same time," said Gramps. "I think it will be best if we go somewhere away from the village to try the machine properly without the added stress of people we know being involved. I am still very concerned that Mr. Higgins walked up to the scarecrow instead of Mr. Pepperdean. Can you do me a huge favour, Reuben?"

"Yeah, what's that?"

"Can you go round and see Mr. Higgins, and ask him a few questions to make sure his brain hasn't been damaged."

"What?"

"As a scientist, I need to give his cognitive skills a quick test, I'll give you a list of questions. The machine is switched off and there won't be any interference with his brain now, so you *should* be safe."

Reuben knocked on Mr. Higgins' door and nervously waited.

The door flew open, "Yes!" said Mr. Higgins, rather impatiently.

"Who are you?" asked Reuben, looking up from the sheet of paper.

"Shouldn't I be asking you that?" Mr. Higgins said, glaring at him. "I am Sir Jeffrey Higgins, QC!"

"What year did the second World War end?" Reuben asked.

"Nineteen forty-five!"

"It's good that your brain isn't frazzled after all," said Reuben. "Enjoy the rest of your day, sir."

"Phew!" said Gramps. "I was worried that he might have brain damage. Thanks for doing that Reuben, although it would have been good if you could have read him all the questions."

"It was obvious he was alright, and he was very touchy, and becoming angry again."

"I think we'll have a day out in London, and I'll take the machine there, well away from anyone we know. In fact, I'll treat you and your friend Simon. I'll buy your train tickets and pay for all other expenses. I fancy being generous."

"Wow, that's really kind of you Gramps," said Reuben. "What brought the generosity on? I'll ring Simon. I'm sure he'll go, especially if you're paying for everything. He'll be fascinated with your Mind Machine, he's always been really interested in science."

"Make sure he's the only one who knows about my machine. I know you won't be able to help yourself in telling Simon, but I suppose it won't do that much harm, as long as he doesn't tell anyone else. I must admit he does seem like a sensible lad. While we're up in London. I'll treat you both to the Dentures Museum. It has false teeth dating from before Queen Victoria's time. You can see the original plaque and dried gunge."

"Can't we go somewhere a bit more exciting?" groaned Reuben. "And a bit more pleasant?"

"You should be grateful I'm treating you!" snapped Gramps. "Everything in life can't be exciting. That's the problem with you youngsters, you expect fun on tap. The discipline of doing something you don't want to do will do you good!"

"Huh, some treat," huffed Reuben.

"That's another problem with you youngsters," said Gramps. "You are all so ungrateful!"

# Chapter Three

## Back at School

"Oi!" shouted Mr. Horns. "Get on with your experiment Reuben!"

Reuben felt confused as he walked about the science lab trying to look busy. All his peers were already in their groups of three and now he felt alone in this crowded science lab. He knew no one wanted him in their group. He had missed so many science lessons, he had no idea what was going on. Even his best friend Simon was already in a group with John and Julie, all with their heads down, knowing exactly what to do and getting on with their experiment.

"Your grandfather might be a Professor of Neuroscience, but it certainly hasn't been passed down to you!" blasted Mr. Horns, staring at Reuben. "You are utterly USELESS!" he bellowed. "GET OUT OF MY CLASSROOM AND GO AND SEE THE

HEAD TEACHER AND TELL HIM HIM YOU ARE
A WASTE OF SCHOOL SPACE!"

Reuben could clearly see the crumbs in Mr. Horns'
beard and plaque in between his brown bottom teeth,
and smell a whiff of foul breath as his teacher shouted
at him. Then as he raised his arms in the air, a fierce
stench like rotten onions burst forth from the holes
under the arms of his tweed jacket. "GO ON, GET
OUT!" he shouted.

Reuben felt relieved to be out of the mass
confusion of the science lesson, but now felt even
more petrified at the thought of going to see the Head
Teacher, Mr. Pride.

Reuben stood outside the light wood door and
desperately tried to pluck up the courage to knock.
Written on a large plaque on the door was: HEAD
TEACHER THE HONOURABLE MR. PRIDE. BA
(Ed) (Honours) I.A.M. G.R.E.A.T. (Honours)

Reuben had already been bellowed at very loudly
by Mr. Pride, for missing two weeks of exams only a
week ago, and now he had to face him all over again.
He just mustered up all his courage, lifted his knuckles
and knocked on the door. His heart pounded. The
door quickly opened and Mr. Pride stood there in his
usual immaculate dark pinstripe suit with a folded
white handkerchief poking up from his top pocket.

"YES!" he grunted, staring right into Reuben's eyes.

"Mr. Horns told me to come to see you and say
you are a waste of school space."

"WHAT?" That's it Oxley. You are excluded from this great school for the rest of the day. GET OUT!"

Reuben was deep in thought, as he walked home. He hated school more and more each day, especially since a few weeks ago, when he had been sent to the school Psychologist, Mrs Brown, to find out what the school could do to improve his attendance and make him concentrate more when he was there. Reuben had asked if he could be put on a three day week, and she suddenly exploded with anger and sent him to Mr. Pride. He just paced up and down his office, shouting: "What about me? My reputation is at stake! You make me look bad! You make my school look bad!

Reuben's best friend Simon was clever when he could be bothered. His father was a doctor, and they lived in the biggest house in the village. Simon was top of the class even without even having to work hard.

Reuben fancied Julie, a pretty blonde girl in his class, but now she was going out with John Johnson the local bully, he felt even more fed up with school. 'How could she go out with such an oaf as Bully Johnson instead of someone nice, like me?' he always thought. He realized he was a bit shy, but if only she would give him a chance. The sight of Bully Johnson kissing her between fag drags around the back of the bike sheds made him feel sick. 'It should be me kissing her lovely fresh red lips, not that bullying oaf who never even cleans his teeth,' he would think. Reuben dreamed of one day being a mega famous rock star on a big stage, performing a lightning fast guitar solo, his fingers whizzing all over the fret board of his Fender guitar, and girls screaming; some jumping on to the stage, and having to be to be carried off by big burly security guards.

A car hooting loudly snapped him out of his daydream. It was his form teacher Mr. Horns, in his red Nissan Micra, slowing right down. "You idiot!" he bellowed. "I was threatened with the sack over you wrongly telling Mr. Pride that I told you to tell him that HE was a waste of school space. And now I'm late for my doctor's appointment. I will make your life an utter misery from now on. I shall turn a blind eye to you being bullied."

"You do anyway," said Reuben.

"How dare you answer me back just because you are off school grounds. And stop walking when I'm talking to you!" he bellowed, as he slowly drove his car forward. He then sped off, shaking his head as he went.

# Chapter Four

## A Trip to London

Simon arrived at Reuben's house late as usual. Reuben heard the doorbell and leapt out of bed.

"A free day out in London! Should be a cracker," said Simon, sipping his coffee. He had his hair slightly spiked up hinting the latest fashion, maybe enough to have respect among the bullies. His slim, almost invisible spectacles made him look super intelligent and cool.

"My grandfather's going to pick us up in a minute," Reuben told him. "Don't forget to keep your phone switched off. You know how he gets very angry over mobile phones. We don't want my grandfather to cancel using his machine, do we?"

"What machine?" Simon asked.

"The one I told you about on the phone, remember?"

They stood on the pavement waiting for Gramps to pick them up. A woman wearing a baggy coat and with two panting dogs on leads, staggered past.

A postman with a shaved head and wearing shorts, was flicking through a pile of letters as he crossed the road.

There was a great bang and splutter and Gramps' black Morris Minor came around the corner. Blue smoke billowed up from behind it before it suddenly squeaked to a halt.

"Good grief!" remarked Simon. "Are we going to the station in that?"

They were surprised to see Bert Blundy, the local gardener, sitting in the middle of the back seat.

Bert Blundy was known locally as Blundergutts due to his reputation as the clumsiest and most useless man in the village. He lived in a shed but always wanted to better himself and speak with an upper class accent. In exchange for gardening, Mrs Cottingham, a retired speech and drama teacher, gave him elocution lessons, making him do several exercises. His dirty tie and shirt made him look like a country gent…so he thought.

Seeing that the front seat was taken up with a small suitcase, they both squeezed in the back, either side of Blundergutts.

"Hullo again Simon," greeted Gramps, turning round. "This is my ex gardener. He is known locally as Blundergutts. I don't think you've met him Simon."

"Hi there Blunderbuss, nice to meet you," greeted Simon.

"Blundergutts!" Blundergutts corrected him sternly. "I don't much like the name, but you have to have a thick skin in the gardening industry." His thinning grey and ginger hair looked damp with sweat with a few drops on his forehead. The rather dirty green tweed tie seemed to be almost strangling him. Yooo tooo behaaave yourselves," he suddenly said in a very loud overly posh accent. "Make sure you show respect for your adults," he added, reverting back to his strong country accent, his thin lips moving like two shiny earth worms.

"What are you doing coming to London?" asked Reuben. "You always said you hate London, and would never go there?"

"Well, your grandfather offered to buy my train ticket to show me just how good his new machine is…I have my doubts whether it will work though."

Blundergutts' huge bodily presence in the cramped old classic car made Simon and Reuben feel more and more uncomfortable as they sat, crushed up beside him. The smell of stale clothes wafting from Blundergutts, made Simon feel sick.

The car popped and spluttered as they moved off.

"What on earth is that awful stink?" shouted Gramps, almost swerving into a crowded bus stop. His tyres screeched, sending many villagers running for their lives! "It smells like rotten eggs!"

Reuben grabbed the window handle and frantically wound it round and round, but there was just a loud squeaking sound and the dirty window remained stationary.

Simon tried his handle, but the same thing happened.

"I'm afraid the windows are all jammed," said Gramps. "It's on my to-do list to get them fixed."

The windows started steaming up, and Gramps grabbed an old sock to wipe the windscreen.

Simon opened his door in desperation.

"You can't get out yet!" snapped Gramps. "We're doing over twenty-five miles an hour and we're nowhere near the station!"

"I just needed fresh air!" gasped Simon, closing the door again. "It's so hot in here!"

"Stop the car for goodness sake, Gramps!" Reuben called out, now with his shirt over his face.

"We can't or we'll miss the train," Gramps snapped.

"How-now-brown-cow!" Blundergutts repeated in a loud, strange, overly posh voice while reading from his book entitled 'Speak Like a Lord in a Week'.

"I hope you're all interested in dentures," interrupted Gramps, peering into the small rear-view mirror.

"Er...what?" said Simon.

"He might take us to a Dentures Museum," Reuben told him. "Unless we can persuade him to take us to something a bit more interesting."

"Somewhere else more interesting won't be difficult," said Simon. "One of my uncles worked at the Dentures Museum as an attendant for a couple of weeks, until he suddenly collapsed and had to be rushed to hospital."

"Oh, dear me," said Gramps. "What was the matter with him?"

"They put it down to chronic boredom," replied Simon. "Apparently, he still sometimes wakes up in the middle of the night screaming 'I'm so bored, get me out of here.'"

"Oh dear me," replied Gramps again, as he crunched the gear stick into second then slowed to a halt. "I can't see out of the rear window to park, it's too steamed up. Take this and give it a wipe," he said to Reuben, handing him an old ragged pair of underpants.

"Yuk!" grunted Reuben, reluctantly taking hold of them with his thumb and forefinger. He found the courage to bunch the pants up in his hand and turned round and wiped the condensation-covered rear window.

The car spluttered and popped as Gramps reversed it into a parking space.

"This is miles away from the station," remarked Reuben.

"Don't exaggerate, it's only about half a mile away," said Gramps. "The station car park will be full up by now. Besides, it's five pounds a day and it's free here."

Blundergutts wheezed loudly as they slowly walked along the road to the station.

"Slow down, I can't keep up!" he wheezed, his wellington boots thundering and squeaking as he plodded along behind them.

"You'll have to try to lose some weight," said Gramps.

"What, now?"

The pedestrian lights beeped and they walked across the road to Haywards Heath Station. Rows of taxis lined up waiting for their fares. There was a tiny florist shop, with stacks of flowers outside.

Reuben always loved the distinctive smell of train buildings and platforms and couldn't wait to ride on a train again. They stood back as Gramps waited in the queue to buy the tickets.

"Make the most of this treat, it's never going to happen again," he said, magnanimously handing them each a ticket.

They walked up the long slope towards the steps to the platforms above.

"Wait for me!" puffed Blundergutts, as he thundered along behind them, with sweat now pouring down his face. He was wheezing so loudly, as they walked up the steps to platform 3, that Reuben was worried sick that Blundergutts might collapse. "Are you alright?" he asked him.

Blundergutts just stared at him, as he gasped for air, while still plodding along in his wellington boots.

"Why didn't your grandfather drop me off first?" he gasped. "He knows I find it difficult and painful to walk very far, especially trying to keep up with fast walkers."

"Why does everyone call him Blundergutts?" hissed Simon to Reuben. "I've seen him around the village. He lives in a shed doesn't he?"

"He does live in a shed, but he's quite a nice chap," whispered Reuben. "But everything seems to go wrong for him, and he's very clumsy. That's why he has the nick name of Blundergutts. In fact his real name is Bert Blundy."

They stood on the platform. The rails started buzzing and a fast express train raced through the station whipping up wind as it shot past. A serviette rose up in the air followed by a centre spread of a newspaper flapping almost like a bird before dropping down in between the railway tracks once again.

Blundergutts pulled his book out again. "Peter Piper Picked a peck of pickled peppers!" he called out in a dramatic voice trying to improve his tone and diction of speech with this particular exercise.

"How now brown cow feeding on the green green grass!" he said even louder, still peering at his book.

"What's the matter with him? I think he's mad!" gasped Simon. "He keeps going on about brown cows and pickled peppers in that hideous fake posh voice. Just what is he on about? I can't stand this all day, it's so embarrassing, especially with people looking."

"He's training to be posh," said Reuben.

"Really?"

"Yes," replied Reuben. "Those exercise books have rhymes and words to help someone pronounce things more clearly and poshly."

They clambered on to the nine-thirty-two to London Victoria.

They all sat down on the blue patterned seats. The train jerked forward and slowly moved out of the station. A man with sparse hair scraped across his balding head and wearing an immaculate black suit and dark blue tie, sat opposite Blundergutts. He was reading a Times Newspaper. He coughed slightly, looked up briefly then carried on looking over his half spectacles at his paper.

"I wonder if he started life as a gardener?" said Blundergutts.

"Shush!" hissed Gramps. "Please don't start talking stupid now."

The man looked up again and stared over his half spectacles at Blundergutts. Then his eyes slowly glanced down at Blundergutts' wellington boots.

They all clambered off the train and on to a crowded Victoria Station. Gramps struggled along with his old leather suit case under his arm.

"Ah Hullo Ted! Fancy seeing you here!" said Gramps, surprised to see his local log man slowly walking along, looking well out of place in the sea of people, all heading for the station exit. His trilby hat looked like a flowerpot perched on his head. He had a tanned face like an old strip of crinkly leather. He was short, hunched over slightly and was wearing a seriously creased grey suit and dull brown shoes. He was carrying a large disc-shaped case under each arm. "Er 'ullo Professor," he said in his usual low gruff voice.

"Hullo! What on earth are you doing up in London?" Gramps asked him. "I almost didn't recognise you in clean smart clothes. And what are those big plate-shaped things you're carrying?"

"Nosy, aren't you?" mumbled Ted.

"When are you going to deliver me more logs?" continued Gramps angrily. "I paid you for a full load last winter and you gave me less than three quarters of a load. And my neighbour said that he thought the sacks of logs which he bought felt light, and lo and behold, you filled the bottom half with loads of screwed up newspaper!"

"It looked like a load to me," grunted Ted. "I decide 'ow many logs to put in a sack. Anyway, I 'aven't time to talk now, I'm off to play the cymbals in a very impor'ant concert."

"Oh, I didn't know you played music. So it's cymbals you're carrying."

"Yeah, I've learned to play the cymbals," said Ted. "The conductor who is one of my logs customers, 'as given me the part of a big cymbal crash in the middle of a very impor'ant piece of music at a concert today.

If I prove myself to be good, I'll be given another place in next month's even bigger concert."

"Oh, how interesting!" mused Gramps with his hand on his chin. "I bet you don't swindle him with fewer logs in the load! Anyway, which concert is it you're playing at today?"

"The Victoria Symphony Orchestra. It's at the Victoria Concert Hall. It's a charity concert. It's free to members of public. I ain't a member of public of course, but there is a donation box at the back, for public like you."

"Oh, I think we'll come along and give a fellow villager moral support," said the Professor.

"Oh yeah…you lot coming to look at me?" said Ted, perking up a bit. "You'll see me alright as I've got a big proud seat just be'ind the first violins on the front row."

"We'll see you alright don't you worry about that, ha, ha, ha, ha," laughed Gramps.

"What's so funny?" grumbled Ted.

"Nothing."

"Why's he talking to old Ted?" moaned Reuben. "Ted's the biggest con-man in the village. The amount of people he's swindled with his logs is unbelievable. It's a pity there isn't someone else selling logs nearby, an honest person."

"I know where we are going to try out this machine," laughed Gramps, walking back over to them.

"Where?" asked Reuben.

"The Victoria Concert Hall. It's only just up the road. We can easily walk there. That idiot Ted is playing in a concert. He's only got one cymbal crash to make and I'll make sure it's well and truly in the wrong place…it'll be a bit complex but a great test for my machine, and he deserves it because he gave me less than three quarters of a load of logs, but charged me for a full load. I didn't notice until it was too late."

"Is that all we are going to use the machine for today?" groaned Reuben.

"Look, it's up to me what we do with MY machine," retorted Gramps. "What a fantastic blessing we bumped into Ted! He might have got away with doing something successful, we couldn't have that could we, ha, ha, ha, ha," he laughed. "Especially after swindling so many villagers with his logs."

# Chapter Five

## The Concert

"I hope we get a good seat," said Blundergutts, his wellington boots thundering as they walked into the concert hall. Rows of very smartly dressed people sat there on the velvety red seats.

"There's some seats along the back row over there," said Simon.

"Blast! I've lost 'Speak like a Lord in a Week'!" groaned Blundergutts, tapping his pockets. "It must have fallen out of my pocket on the train."

"Thank goodness for that!" chorused Simon and Reuben in unison.

They all squeezed their way along a crowded row and sat down on the comfy seats.

"Are you sure you'll be able to get a clear shot to his head from here!" said Blundergutts, his voice echoing around the concert hall.

Several people looked round, including musicians sitting down below in the spotlit musicians' area.

"Keep your voice down!" hissed Gramps, struggling to hold the machine. He had now removed it from the suitcase and had a large black plastic bin liner draped over it. He pushed the empty suitcase down in front of Reuben's and Simon's feet. Gramps was desperately trying not to accidentally hit the lady next to him with his elbow as he pulled the sack partially off the machine and secretly started fiddling about with it.

"There's Ted sitting over there!" Reuben pointed out.

Ted sat there, in a hunched position just behind the row of first violins. His chin stuck out and his nose looked even longer under the spotlights. His arms were outstretched like a photo of someone doing a star jump, with a large cymbal in each hand.

"He looks so stupid sitting there like that," remarked Reuben.

"I feel sorry for him," said Gramps. "Humping logs all his life, and now he thinks he can suddenly do something really intelligent and skilful. Oh no, no, no, no, even though he's highly unlikely to succeed anyway, I'll make sure he fails."

"SHUUUSH! Please!" the lady next to Gramps hissed with a finger over her mouth. "They're about to start." Her beautifully styled short dark hair, thick framed spectacles and deep red lipstick gave her an air of sophistication and importance.

The conductor stood up. His long frizzy white hair hung down over his eyes like an Old English Sheep Dog. He pointed the baton at a musician who rose to his feet and bowed proudly then held up a small triangle dangling on a string: he then hit it with a small rod and a soft ding sounded around the hall.

A loud belch suddenly burst from Blundergutts' mouth, echoing even louder around the hall, drowning out the sound of the triangle.

"What the dickens!" said the conductor, staring up at the audience. "Let's start again!" He again pointed his baton to the man holding the triangle, who stood up again and struck the triangle which rang out uninterrupted this time. The orchestra burst into life. Circular rows of very serious looking musicians played their instruments with great zest. The trombones and trumpets sounded almost too loud.

Ted just sat there, his eyes blinking nervously as he stared at the conductor, anxious not to miss his cue, his arms still outstretched, ready for action.

Gramps rummaged his hands under the sack and switched on the machine.

The music abruptly ceased as quickly as it had started.

An elegant lady in a long blue dress, long blond hair, and bright pink lipstick proudly walked out on to the stage below. Everyone clapped loudly.

She then raised her arms towards the vaulted ceiling and opened her mouth wide. The beautiful sound of her voice echoed around the hall as she started to sing.

Gramps was so struck with her beautiful voice, he accidentally pressed the speech button with his elbow along with the volume slide to 'very loud'. The electronic posh lady's voice piped up from the machine. "GOOD AFTERNOON, THE MACHINE IS READY NOW. PLEASE TAP IN A MESSAGE, OR WOULD YOU RATHER USE RANDOM ACCESS BRAINS?"

Gramps tried to ignore the glares from people all around him and desperately fumbled his fingers around under the black sack to cancel the speech, but accidentally hit a couple of other buttons. "THANK YOU FOR CONTINUING," the electronic lady's voice piped up again. "RANDOM ACCESS BRAINS IS NOW IN OPERATION. UNFORTUNATELY THERE IS A SLIGHT MALFUNCTION AND ONLY ONE RANDOM WORD FROM THE ELECTRONIC DICTIONARY CAN BE SAID IN UNISON BY THE AFFECTED BRAINS."

Several people sitting in front of the machine suddenly stood up together in the hall. They all started droning in a loud deep harmony together. "Trash! Trash! Trash! Trash!"

The opera singer burst into tears and hurried off the stage.

The conductor dropped his baton in shock as the orchestra ground to a halt. "If that's what you lot think of us…please leave now," he called up to the group of standing spectators.

Gramps banged his hand down on the cancel button that he'd now fixed, and the group of people stopped droning and slowly sat down again.

The lady's voice piped up. "MEGA PERSONALITY CHANGE MODE IS NOW IN OPERATION AND INSTALLING : 'I AM A ROCK STAR.'"

Gramps frantically fumbled his hands about, desperately trying to cancel this very dangerous mode he had created and forgotten about. The cancel button shot off and fell on the floor. To his horror, he then heard the ping of the extra strong waves being sent out and he saw the machine was aimed straight at the conductor who suddenly stood still.

The orchestra fumbled a bit and slowed down as they saw no directions coming from their now static conductor, but managed to keep playing. His tongue flicked in and out, as he violently nodded his head up and down, swooshing his long hair about from side to side. He suddenly grabbed a cello from a startled lady. He fell to his knees, and continued flicking his tongue in and out, his eyes looking wild. Reuben and Simon were in hysterics.

Gramps just managed to find the cancel button and pushed it back into position. He banged his fist down on it repeatedly in sheer desperation.

The conductor stood up. "Why did you give me this?" he shouted, handing the cello back to the horrified lady. He shook his head several times, staggered to a seat and sat down.

Seeing a problem, the orchestra now fell completely silent.

The conductor rose to his feet again. "I don't know what went wrong there! Get your act together you lot!" he added sternly to the musicians as he picked up his baton from the floor.

"What's happening?" said Reuben. "Give me the machine Gramps! – you're making a pig's ear of the whole thing."

"I know my machine!" replied Gramps, crossly.

"I don't think you need to waste the batteries on old Ted, he's as thick as two of his logs," said Blundergutts. "I think we should just get out of here, fast!"

"Will you lot up there stop talking! You're putting my musicians off!" the conductor shouted to the audience. "Anyway, just listen to the music! We've put in weeks of practice for today."

"Yes! Shush, will you lot stop being so selfish!" said the lady next to Gramps. "If you want to talk, go outside…please!"

"Yes," agreed a posh-looking gentleman, the other side.

The conductor ran the back of his hand over his sweaty forehead, causing the baton to briefly point in Ted's direction.

Even though there was no music being played, seeing this as a signal to make a big clash of the cymbals, Ted suddenly rose proudly to his feet and opened his arms even wider, ready for the great cymbal clash. He was stooped over so much that in front of him, the seated violinist's head was in between the cymbals. A set of false teeth flew out of the violinist's mouth as the cymbals whacked him on the ears. "OOOOOOOooooooo!" he gasped, dropping his violin.

"Ha, ha, ha," laughed Gramps to Reuben. "And I didn't do any of that, he did that himself, the idiot. I'll soon make sure everyone hears it next time, ha, ha, ha." He then switched on a small torch, put his head under the sack and started tapping in a message.

"Will you lot please be quiet! For goodness sake!" snapped a man turning round from his seat just in front of them.

"What are you doing now?" hissed the lady next to Gramps, looking down at him as his head moved about under the sack. He tapped in the message which said: 'Stand up and clash your cymbals now.'

The conductor waved his baton about and the orchestra burst into life again, and the opera singer reappeared, opened her mouth wide and began to sing again.

Gramps quickly heaved the machine up and lent it on the shoulder of the man sitting in front of him and stared through the riflescope. He lined up the cross hairs with Ted's head and then moved his finger towards the action button, waiting for the right moment.

"Get off! What's that? A gun?" snapped the man, jerking his shoulder up and making Gramps hit the action button straight away.

Ted suddenly stood up, opened his arms wide again and clashed the cymbals together with a terrific crash, which reverberated around the concert hall.

"I've done enough now," muttered Gramps, wrapping the black plastic sack around the machine. "Let's just enjoy the music."

There was peace for everyone at last as they all sat quietly for the next half an hour, enjoying the music.

The concert drew to a close, and the hall erupted in applause.

"I've got something to say!" called out the conductor. "From the remote village of Ardingly, Mr. Ted Smells is a woodsman. Only a year ago, he started having lessons in percussion, specializing in the cymbals, and I gave him the opportunity to play the cymbals in my concert. I instructed him to clash the cymbals on the beat of the fifty-fifth line. But the composer of this great work, Ludwick Van Rumpstaken, wrote the piece for the cymbals to be clashed a quarter of a fraction of a beat just behind the one quiet note from the oboe. Only the very greatest percussionists have ever been able to do this, but Mr. Ted Smells did it here today! I don't know how, but he did. For this I bow to him as a great man. He is a very talented percussionist indeed."

The whole hall again erupted in loud resounding

applause and cheers, and Ted slowly rose to his feet and bowed.

"Blast, I've accidentally made Ted a hero," shouted Gramps. "I'll soon put an end to that!"

"No, leave him be," called back Reuben. "Let the poor man enjoy the moment. At least you managed to find out how good the machine is."

"You're absolutely right," shouted Gramps, above the continuing loud cheers and applause. "I don't usually listen to you, but this time I think you're absolutely right. I don't know what came over me. That's what worries me about this machine. Even *I* got carried away. Actually I think I've done enough with it today! Let's go back to Ardingly and I'll treat you all to supper at The Greyhound Inn. They do cheesy chips with egg and bacon on top for only four ninety-nine each, and it's absolutely delicious!"

"That's a great idea," agreed Reuben. "Especially now we don't have to go to that awful boring dentures museum."

"Thanks for reminding me, we must visit the museum, it's only around the corner," replied Gramps. "Don't forget I've agreed to treat you all to a snack later. And it's about time you two did something you don't want to do for a change!"

"I'm well impressed with your Grandpa's machine, he must be so clever," said Simon to Reuben as they walked along the busy road towards the Dentures Museum.

The old red brick building made Reuben and Simon feel sick with boredom even before they entered the Museum. The musty smell hit them as they walked in. Blundergutts' wellington boots boomed and squeaked on the shiny grey floor. Glass cases filled with various false teeth were all around the hall. A group of people stood in the corner listening to a man with a grey suit, short pointed grey beard, grey hair and a twisted looking mouth.

"Let's go and hear what he has to say-we might learn something," said Gramps.

Reluctantly, they followed him over to join the group. There were several people standing around the museum guide. One very serious-looking lady particularly stood out. She had thick glasses, green tweed jacket and was leaning heavily on a walking stick.

The museum guide paused for a moment, then carried on in his dull boring voice. "False teeth were invented to take the place of teeth which had fallen out or had to be removed," he said.

"Really?!" said Blundergutts aloud.

The Museum guide looked fiercely at Blundergutts, then continued. "These false teeth were quite good, but the fit was often poor, and back then, there were no adhesive products to bond the teeth plates, so people had to use their mouths to keep the teeth sucked into position. When people spoke, the teeth would often remain stationary while the lips moved which er…"

"Made them look stupid," interrupted Blundergutts, trying to be helpful.

"I don't need your help giving my speech!" blasted the Museum guide. "I have been doing these tours for over twenty years and everything I say is highly articulate sense, and you seem to talk nonsense! Now just be quiet and listen to me, like everyone else does!"

Blundergutt' right foot squeaked forward as his wellington slipped on the shiny floor and he accidentally kicked the lady's walking stick from under her.

"AAAARGH!" she shouted as she went down. Her teeth bit into the handle of the walking stick as she hit the floor, the stick clattering loudly on the hard surface, her handbag flying open spilling handkerchiefs, chap sticks, a brush, a small tin of Vaseline and and a thick purse.

"Good heavens above! Are you alright" called out the Museum guide.

"You alright?" added Blundergutts offering his arm to help her up.

"Get off, just leave me in peace! You clumsy oaf!" she shouted to Blundergutts, staring up at him intently through her thick glasses, as she stayed on all fours. "I nearly lost my front teeth biting on to my stick. They feel all achy now," she said, spitting some dust from her mouth. "And I think they might be a bit loose!"

"I'm sure they'll tighten up after a few days," said Blundergutts. "Anyway, if not, there's enough spare false teeth here for you. Surely him with the beard will give you a pair; give them a quick rinse under a tap and they'll be alright, I'm sure."

"How dare you make light of it!" snapped the lady still down on her knees. "Someone help me up for heaven's sake!" she called out. "Just standing there like a load of nosy spectators!"

Several people suddenly rushed over and carefully helped her up. "I'm alright, I'm alright!" she snapped to the group of people. Now she was safely up, she pushed away their helpful arms and hands and started to brush herself down.

Blundergutts then accidentally kicked the case with a terrific bang, and just managed to stay on his feet.

"Blundergutts!" shouted Gramps angrily, picking up the case.

The machine suddenly burst into life.

"ACCESS BRAINS HAS NOW BEEN INSTITUTED!" came the loud but slightly muffled ladies voice from inside the suit case . ONE WORD TAKEN FROM THE DICTIONARY WILL BE RANDOMLY DISTRIBUTED INTO THE AFFECTED BRAIN AND REPLACE ONE OTHER WORD. THANK YOU.

"Practise your ventriloquist skills elsewhere!" spat the guide. "Just stop it and let me finish speaking! Right, where was I? Ah yes, I'll start at the beginning after all these very rude interruptions." He suddenly paused and his face went very pale, his mouth dropping open slightly, his eyes looking very vague. "Early false bosoms were invented to take the place of bosoms which had fallen out. These bosoms were quite good but the fit was often poor, as back in those days, there were no adhesive products to bond the plates, so people had to used their mouths to keep the bosoms sucked into position. When people spoke, the bosoms would often remain stationary while the lips moved. Often people would lack confidence in giving a broad smile with a mouth full of false bosoms."

Everyone just stared in disbelief at the Museum guide.

"Let's go home, I've had enough now," said Gramps to Reuben. "Once Blundergutts gets a bee in his bonnet about something, he gets more and more argumentative. And he's just so clumsy. And I must fix the machine's wretched one word choosing, and it shouldn't have just come on like that even if it was kicked by a thick idiot's size twelve wellington boot!"

"I think you are a very rude man," said Blundergutts to the Museum guide. "I didn't come all the way here to learn about false bosoms! I don't think it will be long before you lose *your* teeth."

"Get out of my museum!" bellowed the museum attendant to Blundergutts.

"I agree, you're causing nothing but unrest!" snapped the lady with the thick glasses and walking stick. "You're making the poor old guide confused and I'm aching all over, including my teeth and gums. In fact as I run my tongue along my teeth, I can feel a slight difference, as if they've moved slightly, I'll have to have an inspection from my dentist."

"I could have a quick look if you like?" said Blundergutts, walking over.

"You keep your filthy fingers away from my mouth, you horrible man," snapped the lady. "Just leave me in peace to enjoy the museum tour."

"Come on, let's go," said Gramps, grabbing Blundergutts' arm.

# Chapter Six

## Another Horrid Day at School

Reuben and Simon burst through the double doors and rushed into the school assembly hall. They walked around, desperately trying to find an empty seat as quickly as possible.

Mr. Pride, the head teacher rose to his feet. "Who are these two late-comers?" he shouted, (knowing full well who they were).

"Er. Reuben Oxley," answered Reuben, sheepishly looking up at Mr. Pride.

"Er. Simon Hadley," spluttered Simon, his face crimson with embarrassment.

"BOTH COME UP HERE NOW!" shouted Mr. Pride.

Reuben and Simon hurriedly walked up on to the stage where the entire teaching staff was seated.

"We have Mr. Bull, an inspector, here today.

LOOK AT HIM WHEN I'M TALKING ABOUT HIM!" bellowed Mr Pride.

Reuben and Simon could hardly see Mr. Bull's eyes through his thick spectacles. His bald head was so shiny it seemed to reflect the summer sunshine streaming through the nearby window.

Mr. Pride, as usual, looked immaculate with his polished complexion, neat swept back hair and very expensive looking dark pinstripe suit, with a neatly folded handkerchief poking from his top pocket. Reuben felt petrified, standing up there in front of the whole school. All eyes were now on him and Simon.

"You two are an utter disgrace!" Mr. Pride continued, at the top of his voice.

"That's right!" agreed the Inspector. "These lads need to be disciplined as an example to the whole school. Lateness should not be tolerated!"

"Quite right," Mr. Pride agreed smugly, feeling pleased that he'd impressed the school Inspector. "Your teacher Mr. Horns will deal with you two later. Go and stand at the back of the hall!"

Reuben had the usual horrible feeling that always overwhelmed him when he walked into the classroom. Just the thought of going to this school always made his stomach churn. Horrible teachers and bullies seemed to be everywhere. The teachers nearly always shouted at him, rather than talk to him normally. The Headteacher, Mr. Pride, had told his Aunt that if he didn't start working at school soon he would end up leaving at the age of sixteen with no qualifications, and find it very difficult to get a decent job, let alone go to college or university. Reuben knew this was probably true, but making a fresh start was so difficult after doing virtually nothing, apart from daydreaming through each lesson for the last nine years. Like Reuben, Simon could never seem to get to school on time.

Mr. Horns, their teacher, was standing in the classroom, waiting for them.

"SIT DOWN!" he bellowed.

Reuben and Simon hurriedly pulled out their chairs and sat down. The other pupils looked on in silence, waiting, with relish, for Mr. Horns to give Reuben and Simon a good 'telling off'.

"You have utterly disgraced me in front of the head teacher, and if that isn't bad enough, in front of the school Inspector! Both of you apologise now!"

"We're very sorry," they both said in unison.

"I'm afraid sorry is not good enough. It's too late! Just be quiet! Why can't you be normal Reuben? You Simon, are very clever, so why just blow it all by hanging around with Reuben? In fact, you and Reuben have both got two weeks' detention starting from today."

"But I have things to do!" Simon protested.

"For answering me back you'll both get an extra week's detention," shouted Mr. Horns with bits of breakfast pinging from his soggy lips, which protruded from his grey bushy beard. He always wore the same old tweed jacket that he'd worn for years and every time he raised his arms, a strong smell like rotting onions would fill the classroom.

Mr. Pride, the headmaster, suddenly came strolling in. "Everything all right, Mr. Horns?"

"Oh yes, Mr. Pride," said Mr Horns, almost bowing.

"Very well, but make sure you severely punish Reuben and Simon. I'd rather see them receive too much punishment than not enough. It's a great shame caning has been abolished. See you later in the staff room, Horns."

"Oh yes, sir…I've brought some 'extra shine' shoe polish to do your shoes later, sir."

"Listen to that grovelling sucker," hissed Simon.

"Yes," murmured Reuben in agreement.

"What? I heard you, Simon. You just called me a grovelling sucker! And you Reuben agreed!" shouted Mr. Horns. "Don't even try to deny it. You two will have quadruple maths twice over. You will do VERY difficult equations ALL day AND for an hour AFTER school. AND to watch over you during school time to make sure you THINK hard and keep WORKING, I will put John Johnson in charge of you."

"What?" gasped Reuben. "Not Bully Johnson. He keeps thumping us in the face for no reason!"

"Good, good, ha! ha!" sneered Mr. Horns. "I like the sound of that."

"It's illegal for him to thump us!" Simon protested.

"I give him full permission to thump you …I MAKE THE RULES IN MY CLASSROOM. IS THAT CLEAR!?" bellowed Mr. Horns, as lots more thick saliva mixed with egg pinged across the classroom, a piece of which hit Simon right in the corner of his eye.

Reuben could again clearly see Mr. Horns' brown bottom teeth with yellowy gunge in-between, it made him feel sick. And there was an even more putrid stench of foul breath than usual.

Bully Johnson rose to his feet and walked purposefully towards them. He was the tallest boy in the class. His face wore a constant smirk, showing greenish, snaggly teeth, and he had Indian ink hand-written tattoos all over his hands and up his neck. His hair was almost shaved off. "Get wor'ing you two cre'ins!" he growled, clenching his fists, enjoying his moment of power.

"We haven't been given any sums yet!" Reuben replied. "Ouch!" he shouted, as bully Johnson's fist bounced off his cheek.

Mr. Pride flung open the door and strode in again. "Did I just see you punch Reuben in the face?" he said to Bully Johnson.

"Er…yeah, I suppose so," replied Bully Johnson.

"Well done, keep up the good work," said Mr Pride. "Right. The Inspector, Mr. Bull, who was here last week and this morning, is so impressed with my school that he has told the Chief Inspector about us and he is coming to visit us this Thursday, which is the day after tomorrow. I think a top award is definitely lined up for me...so arrive ON TIME YOU TWO!" he bellowed, staring intently at Simon and Reuben. "I've probably already lost a couple of marks off my very already high score today because of YOU TWO! I want all your best behaviour on Thursday, is that clear?"

"Yes, sir," the whole class murmured nervously.

"An award for you, sir, would be marvellous. You deserve it," grovelled Mr Horns.

The bell rang for break time. The classroom erupted in noise as chairs were pulled out and everyone scrambled for the door.

"I can't stand this!" hissed Simon. "I can't stand Bully Johnson! How could Julie go out with a ghastly person like that?"

"Look! Now Bully Johnson has gone for a fag break, let's escape from here," said Reuben, rushing to the open window.

"Great idea! I'm right behind you," agreed Simon.

They climbed through the open window, and jumped down on to the ground. They ran between some thick bushes, then across the edge of the playing field, to avoid being seen from the school. A football match was taking place the other side of the field. A distant whistle sounded as someone fell over during a tackle, then another whistle as the ball went into the back of the net. They kept looking away from the match, and kept their heads down hoping not to be noticed by Mr. Gibbons, the P.E. teacher.

The heat of the sun warmed their backs as they ran through a field of long grass. They climbed over a style and continued along a narrow footpath, which came out almost opposite the road where Gramps lived.

Reuben knocked on the door. After waiting, for what felt like for ages, it slowly creaked open.

"Hi Gramps," greeted Reuben.

"Come in you two," replied Gramps. "Fancy a cooked breakfast?"

"Cor yeah, thanks," replied Reuben and Simon with relish.

Gramps put down two plates on which were two large sausages, a mass of baked beans, a couple of fried eggs and a huge pile of mash. The stained yellow wallpaper and wobbly old pine table and chairs made eating breakfasts here so relaxing and enjoyable for Simon. He didn't have to worry if food fell on the table or on the old dirty black and white squared lino. Simon's mum had always moaned that too many of Reuben's grandfather's breakfasts might give him a heart attack in later life, but that was a long way off at fourteen. Simon looked in shock as Gramps opened his mouth very wide and pushed a quivering, overloaded fork slowly towards his wide-open mouth. Muffin, Gramps' black and white tom cat, that he had got from a rescue sanctuary, stared up at Gramps' overloaded fork. Muffin had only one eye and half his tail missing. A sausage hit the floor. Muffin leapt forward, like a lion going for its prey, and grabbed it, then carried it off, dumped it on the floor and with his head sideways, started to crunch into this easy mouthful.

"That machine is so mega cool," said Simon.

"Yes, it's more than mega cool, it's mega freezing!" said Reuben. "I can't wait to use it again, What about now?"

"No, no, I'm thinking of destroying it," said Gramps. "I feel delighted that I've proved to myself that it was a successful project, but if it got into the wrong hands, it could be disastrous."

# Chapter Seven

## Reuben visits Bert Blundergutts

Reuben squeezed through the gap in the hedge and knocked on Blundergutts' shed door.

"Who's there?" muttered Blundergutts, shaking his razor in a bucket of cold scummy water.

"It's me, Reuben."

Blundergutts rubbed a dirty threadbare towel over his fat face, removing the shaving foam. He quickly forcibly did up some buttons on his stained undersized shirt.

"Come in, my boy," he said, pushing the door open.

"Hi Blundergutts," said Reuben, stepping in as he surveyed the terrible mess. Ragged blue curtains dangled in front of a broken grimy window, and a single light bulb, hanging from the ceiling, was all but obscured by a thick layer of dust and brown burnt cobwebs. Blundergutts' small bed with its lumpy mattress, looked as though it hadn't been made in months, and there was a dirt-ingrained impression of his body on the sheets. Rusty garden tools were strewn carelessly in a corner next to Blundergutts' smelly old trousers, which, to Reuben's shock, stood upright, leaning against the shed wall, with the bottoms of the trouser legs still stuck in the wellington boots.

Despite all the mess, Reuben quite liked visiting Blundergutts in his old shed. It wouldn't be long now before the huge tin of chocolates was opened.

"I feel really down in the dumps today," moaned Blundergutts.

"Why?" asked Reuben. "You seemed in quite good spirits when we went up to London, and using the machine. I actually feel so proud of my grandfather making a potentially world-changing machine like that, all on his own!"

"Yes, but now it's back to reality," groaned Blundergutts. "My last gardening job came to an end yesterday when the lawn mower ran out of control and crashed into Mr. and Mrs. Hopkins' conservatory. They were furious. But the stupid thing is, it wasn't my fault. I tried to turn left and went straight on because of the wet grass."

"Oh," said Reuben, trying hard not to smile.

"This means that I now have no income," moaned Blundergutts. "I haven't a clue where I'm going to live as I won't be able to afford my shed rent, and Stan the landlord has already warned me that he's going to put the rent up next month. I don't think I'm cut out for this life," he groaned. "Everything seems to go wrong. I should have been born an animal or a bird. They don't have worries like us humans."

"I don't know about that," said Reuben. "You might have been born a dog with a cruel owner. But looking on the positive side, I know a way to make you rich, successful and ending up in a dream home."

"How's that?" asked Blundergutts, flicking a tea bag off his spoon and into an already over-flowing rubbish bucket.

"Think! Think! Think!" said Reuben. "It's obvious. You know, my grandfather's machine!"

"I've been thinking about it," said Blundergutts. "I think that Ted Smells just clashed the cymbals anyway. I can't see how that machine worked."

"You might not have faith in it, " said Reuben, "and it does seem far-fetched. But I've seen it working fantastically on Gramps' neighbour. I've no doubt that it works. In fact, it's so simple to use and I couldn't believe the power it has."

Blundergutts listened, now starting to feel more convinced by Reuben's enthusiasm. "Well if it really does work, let's get hold of it," he said. "You know your grandfather is such a boring old man – he'll never use the machine to its full potential. If it really does have the power that you say it has, we could change things to go our way. I could get a very good job and then everyone will respect me and stop looking on me as a useless waste of space."

"The machine is good, but I don't know if it's that good," sniggered Reuben.

"What do you mean?" snapped Blundergutts.

"Only joking," Reuben laughed.

"If it really does work, let's use it now," said Blundergutts. "I could have the wife I want, money I want…I could have it all!"

"Well, there's a slight problem," said Reuben. "Gramps is going to destroy the machine because he thinks, in the wrong hands it could be disastrous. Thinking about it, we might not be able to get hold of the machine without stealing it." he continued. "Do you really want to be still living in a shed in five years' time?"

"I don't want to be living in a shed today, let alone five years time!"

"Well, stop dithering about and help me get hold of the machine!"

"Actually, I've kept it a secret until now, but I know where he keeps a spare machine," continued Blundergutts. "He built two machines together side by side just in case one broke down. He keeps the spare machine under this shed in a sealed box. In fact he was round here a couple of days ago to update it."

"Go and get it now!" said Reuben, rising to his feet. "It's only under this shed, for crying out loud!

I can't believe you've known where the spare machine is and haven't told me. I need to get my hands on it!"

"I'll have to charge you for using it."

"What! Charge me? It doesn't belong to you, it belongs to my grandfather!"

"Look, you know how poor I am, and I've been prepared to share the secret with you. Will a pound an hour be alright?"

"Yes, yes, as long as you give me the spare machine, and if it improves your life, I expect a refund."

"If your grandfather finds out that I've loaned it to you, he'll be very, very angry. I want to supervise you with it too, because if it really does work like you say, it could be dangerous. Anyway, it's time for my afternoon nap. Come back early tomorrow morning and I'll have it all ready for you."

"What! Tomorrow? You're lucky I'm honest, or I'd come back later and get it myself."

# Chapter Eight

## Reuben's Plan of Attack

Reuben returned to Blundergutts' shed bright and early the next morning. He just couldn't wait to start experimenting and doing what he wanted with this replica of his grandfather's new invention. He could make Julie agree to go out with him for starters.

"Great! You've got the spare machine out," said Reuben, staring at it propped up in the corner of the shed. "It's a good job Gramps can't see it just propped up like that with the rusty old tools. I hope it's not switched on!"

"What do you take me for, an idiot?" snapped Blundergutts.

"Well, er, er…anyway, let's get started!"

"I've suddenly had second thoughts," said Blundergutts. "We shouldn't really be doing this. It makes me feel guilty. I think I'll put the machine back in its box and back under my shed. We're tampering with nature. People are designed to think their own thoughts."

"You can't change your mind now," groaned Reuben. "Are you happy with no money and just living in a shed?"

"No, I've told you already, of course not! Would you?"bellowed Blundergutts. "Anyway, I might meet a rich woman. You do have a point though. I have no job and I'm about to be kicked out of my shed because I can't afford the rent. You're right! I'm just going to have to use this machine…if it works."

"Stop saying, 'if it works,' " said Reuben. "This machine is almost certainly identical to the other one, so of course it will work. Have faith! You might meet a rich woman, but without the help of the machine, the meeting is the only thing that will happen, and that will be very brief. Anyway, I have an excellent idea, Blundergutts. My school has an inspection tomorrow. Why don't we sneak into the school early tomorrow morning with the machine, and mess up the whole day so the Inspector realises what a useless headmaster Mr Pride is. Imagine just how much sheer chaos we could cause!"

"There are so many other things we could do with that machine, so why on earth are you choosing the hassle of creeping into your school. We could go to a Ferrari garage and make the salesman give me a Ferrari free of charge."

"Yes, but that wouldn't be as simple as it sounds," said Reuben. "What happens when the Ferrari salesman realises what he has done? It would cause a huge uproar and investigation into how it happened and you would be arrested for theft."

Later, while walking home, Reuben wondered if he should have gone to school that day. After all, he only had a slight headache. He suddenly snapped out of his deep thoughts when he saw Mr Pride, the headmaster, climbing out of a car that had just pulled over.

"You don't look very ill to me!" accused Mr. Pride, looking sternly at Reuben. "I want you in school tomorrow, no matter how ill you are. Even if your stupid Aunt has to bring you in on a stretcher! I want maximum attendance because a top Inspector is visiting us tomorrow."

"I'll see if I'm well enough," croaked Reuben, making his voice sound scratchy.

"If you do not attend tomorrow, I'll see that you are given detention as often as possible and I shall turn a blind eye when you are bullied."

"You do that anyway," Reuben mumbled.

"How dare you answer me back boy! As long as your being bullied doesn't affect ME or the running of MY school, I'm just not interested, is that clear? I'll be off now. See you tomorrow…OR ELSE!"

Simon followed Reuben through the gap in the hedge. "I hope he's in," sighed Reuben.

"Ugh! What a ghastly cramped-looking place to live!" gasped Simon, as Reuben knocked on Blundergutts' shed door.

"Come in," said Blundergutts.

"Don't worry about the mess, he has a huge tin of chocolates," laughed Reuben.

They were soon drinking mugs of tea and eating chocolates while Reuben explained to Blundergutts his plans to disrupt the school inspection.

"Not THE Mr. Horns!" gasped Blundergutts. "Don't say he's still teaching! He taught me, which was over thirty years ago. He was a ghastly man; he didn't like me at all just because I wouldn't do any work. Actually I now think we should teach those teachers a lesson. Fancy allowing you to be thumped, and in the face at that! It's just not right."

"Apparently, the Chief Inspector is coming to visit the school tomorrow," said Reuben. "I've got it all worked out, Blundergutts, how you can be involved without having to meet or be seen by anyone. My grandfather built a fantastic life size replica donkey. One person crouches in the front and the other at the back. Simon and I had a go with it last summer. It was amazing! Once you get a hang of the controls it can do so many things: run, jump, bite if need be…

it's amazing! Anyway, I've got it all worked out. You and Simon will be in the donkey while it stands still in the assembly hall. Everyone will think it's stuffed. It will have a note on it saying that it's a present from Her Majesty the Queen.

"You can't be that stupid, surely," said Blundergutts. "What's the point of me being there as a stuffed donkey? What help will I be like that? But, I suppose it's paid work."

"Yes, alright, I'll pay you," interjected Reuben. "But I want you and Simon there for moral support. You'll be there, but not be there, if that makes sense."

"No it doesn't," moaned Blundergutts.

"Anyway," he continued, "They'll think the donkey's stuffed, so you'll have to keep still. I think that's the best idea. I'll put a note on you to say as I already mentioned, that the donkey's a present from Her Majesty the Queen. If things get really tough, I can load the machine on to your back, and I can jump on and you can gallop out of the hall."

"Well I still think the whole idea is way out of our league," moaned Blundergutts. "Why can't we just do something simple with the machine. This whole idea is ridiculous, but I suppose twenty pounds an hour isn't bad, for just crouching inside a donkey suit."

"What?" gasped Reuben. "Twenty pounds an hour? We'll have to be really quick to keep your cost down! I think we should meet up this evening for a quick rehearsal with the donkey first. Anyway, we might as well go and get it and have another good look at it. I think it's still in a wooden crate in my Gramps' old shed. I know where the key is. I think he eventually intends to break it up for parts anyway. For some unknown reason he thinks it's a terrible failure."

# Chapter Nine

## Practice Makes Perfect

Reuben and Simon met up at seven that evening and managed to creep into Gramps' shed and collect the heavy crate and creep across the overgrown back garden without being seen.

"I hope this is not stealing" puffed Simon.

"No, it's not. It's just borrowing something," Reuben tried to reassure him.

"This is so heavy!" gasped Simon as they staggered along the road towards Blundergutts' shed, carrying the wooden crate between them. "It looks a bit suspicious as well; people are giving us funny looks!"

Back at Bert's shed, they grunted as they all pulled open the crate and then unpacked the big stiff fur donkey suit. "I don't think I can remember how to set it up," said Reuben.

"It's simple. I remember, said Simon. "It was only last summer when we were allowed to try it out. Come on, wake up Reuben!"

"I'm just not wearing that!" Blundergutts muttered, staring at the crumpled donkey suit lying on the floor.

"Come on, you agreed!" said Reuben. "You can't back out now!"

"O.K, I'll try it…but then I'm going to get straight out of it again, or I might insist on even more money."

"What's your middle name, Greedy?" sighed Simon, "You're starting to cost us a fortune and I'M not getting paid."

They helped Blundergutts into the front legs and head of the donkey suit.

"Well, I suppose I'll have to get in the back then," grumbled Simon. "But you owe me one, Reuben."

Simon and Blundergutts were soon inside the hot, stuffy donkey with its huge, floppy ears and slightly twisted face, and lopsided-looking eyes as it staggered and twisted around the garden. "I hope the neighbours aren't looking," came the muffled sound of Blundergutts' voice from inside.

"You need to be zipped up properly!" said Reuben, laughing so much he could hardly stand up. He picked up the large remote control, and pressed the button on which was written: ELECTRONIC ZIP. There was a loud zipping sound followed by a very loud clunk. Reuben then stooped down and rummaged through the crate and pulled out a small brown electronic instruction box. "Here are the electronic instructions! I'll switch it on and it will tell you what to do with the switches which are down inside the hooves," he said in a loud voice so Blundergutts and Simon could hear him. He switched on the machine and a loud posh lady's voice piped up. "WELCOME TO THE MOST ADVANCED ELECTRONIC DONKEY SUIT IN THE WORLD. IF YOU WRIGGLE YOUR FINGERS AROUND, YOU WILL FIND FIVE SWITCHES IN EACH HOOF. I WILL COMMENCE WITH THE FRONT RIGHT HOOF. THE BUTTON TO THE RIGHT IS THE EEYOR BUTTON: PRESS IT NOW."

Blundergutts fumbled around and found the button on the right hand side. He pressed it hard and jumped as the big mouth opened. Daylight flooded in, framed by large yellow square teeth, and there was a deafening and very realistic sound of a braying donkey. "We need blasted ear plugs in here!" Blundergutts shouted. "I'll have to charge more!"

"THE NEXT BUTTON", the lady's voice continued, "IS THE MUNCH BUTTON. BEND DOWN YOUR HEAD SO THAT THE LIPS TOUCH THE GROUND AND ALLOW THE MOUTH TO PRETEND TO MUNCH THE GRASS. THE NEXT BUTTON IS THE MANURE BUTTON. THERE IS A MANURE AND WIND TANK AT THE REAR OF THE DONKEY. THIS IS IN NO WAY MEANT TO BE CRUDE. IT IS TO ENHANCE THE REALISM OF

THE DONKEY. THERE IS NO NEED TO PRESS IT NOW. PLEASE DO NOT TOUCH THE MACHINE-GUN-DUNG-BUTTON UNLESS UNDER SERIOUS THREAT AS IT IS VERY DANGEROUS. IT IS THE SMALL SWITCH BY THE LEFT KNEE JOINT."

"That's enough switch work," said Reuben. "You should have enough functions to work the donkey now."

"Let's get out of here!" groaned Blundergutts in a muffled voice.

Reuben pressed the unzip button but nothing happened. The loud lady's voice piped up again: "I'M AFRAID THERE HAS BEEN A MAJOR MALFUNCTION WITH THE ELECTRONIC ZIP. THE AUTOMATIC REPAIR FUNCTION IS NOW IN OPERATION. THE ZIP SHOULD BE READY TO BE OPENED IN APPROXIMATELY SEVEN DAYS' TIME. SORRY FOR ANY INCONVENIENCE THIS MIGHT CAUSE."

"Inconvenience!" bellowed Blundergutts in a muffled voice. "I will not be a donkey for seven days. Get me out of here now!"

"I can't," said Reuben. "It's jammed. Didn't you hear the lady?"

"Stuff the lady!" bellowed Blundergutts in the muffled voice. "Get me out of here! Cut the blasted thing open with a knife or something, but mind me while you're at it."

"I can't," replied Reuben. "The donkey has a form

of chain-mail inside the false skin to give it added strength. That's why it was so heavy."

"Look…I feel sick!" cried Simon. "Get me out of here. I told my my mum I should be back by eight to have my dinner…just get me out now!"

The false donkey, full of Blundergutts and Simon both panicking and struggling about, was now charging and falling around the garden. It crashed through the hedge and on to the next-door neighbour's lawn. Mr. and Mrs. Johnson could hardly believe their eyes when they saw a mad twisted up donkey rolling around their lawn. "It looks in utter agony!" cried Mrs. Johnson. "It's almost breaking into two. You'd better phone the Animal Hospital. I think it's starting to bray in English!"

The donkey was now rolling around on its back.

"AAAAARRGGHH!!" shouted Simon. "Stop twisting about Blunderbuss!"

"Blundergutts! Not Blunderbuss!" blasted Blunderguts. "The head keeps moving and I can't see out of the blasted eye holes and it's so hot and stuffy!" he continued, as the donkey rolled back through the hedge. "Get the fire brigade to cut us out!"

"What? Phone the fire brigade?" exclaimed Reuben. "They're for emergencies only. Quick! Get into the shed! You're becoming embarrassing. People are starting to stare from their windows!" He grunted as he lifted with all his might to help them back on to their feet and pushed as hard as he could from behind on the cold, stiff fur. Blundergutts could just make out the open shed door through one eye hole. "Steady your blasted legs!" he shouted to Simon.

"I can't see what's happening!" Simon yelled back.

There was a clattering sound as the hooves skidded on the shed floor. The back panel of the shed burst open as the donkey crashed through.

"AAAARGH!" bellowed Blundergutts.

"OOOOFFF!" groaned Simon, as his head crushed up against Blundergutts' huge fat bottom.

The donkey staggered along and rammed into a large shrub.

"OOOOOFF!" gasped Simon as his face rammed up against Blundergutts again.

"Just get us out of this blasted suit NOW!" shouted Blundergutts. "And stop laughing Reuben, it's not funny! I think I might be starting to suffocate!"

"Yes, get us out!" cried Simon. "This terrible smell coming from the front, is getting worse!"

"And you can't be suffocating Blundergutts" said Reuben. "There are little ventilation slots among the fur."

"I'm the judge of whether I'm suffocating or not!" shouted Blundergutts.

The posh lady's voice suddenly piped up again from the remote control unit. "YOU ARE NOW IN A FAVOURABLE POSITION. THE MALFUNCTIONED ZIP HAS BEEN RE-COMMISSIONED AS A CONSEQUENCE OF WHICH, IT WILL NOW OPEN."

"Why can't that stupid woman speak in plain English? What does she mean?" Blundergutts protested. "I can't understand what she's on about! What the blazes does re-commissioned mean?

"She means the zip's working again," mumbled Simon from the back.

Reuben grabbed the remote control unit and pressed the 'zip open' button.

There was a loud zipping sound and Blundergutts and Simon tumbled out onto the ground.

"Isn't it fantastic!" exclaimed Reuben. "It works a treat."

"Fantastic?" moaned Simon sarcastically, rubbing his head. "You should try being trapped in it behind Blunderbuss!"

"Blundergutts!" shouted Blundergutts.

"But it does work a treat," Reuben continued, trying his hardest not to double up with laughter.

"No! It blasted well doesn't work a treat!" shouted Blundergutts, wiping the drops of sweat from his forehead while spitting dust and cobwebs from his mouth.

"I think the zip just needs a bit of oil, that's why it probably jammed," said Reuben. "Anyway, we might as well leave it with you tonight, Blundergutts."

"Well, looking after it for the night," sighed Blundergutts. "You do realise that there'll be a storage fee. And I'll work out the hourly rate for all this."

"Money, money money, that's all you think about!" scolded Reuben. "Which is surprising considering you haven't got any."

"That's why it's all I think about!" blasted back Blundergutts, still wiping sweat from his face.

"Right," said Reuben, "let's all meet up tomorrow morning at seven. That should easily give us enough time to get organised for our great attack on the school tomorrow."

"I'm very worried about this!" groaned Simon. "But if you really feel your plan of ruining the school inspection will work, I suppose I'm in. But have you got a constructive plan organised?"

"Yeah, yeah, it's all in hand, and we have the experience of Captain Blundergutts."

"Who?" spluttered Blundergutts.

"You can be our captain, sir," said Reuben saluting him.

"But…!"

"Good! I'm glad you've agreed!" butted in Reuben. "Let's get the panel of the shed put back, before your landlord sees it."

# Chapter Ten

## The Great Attack

Reuben could hardly sleep for nerves and excitement. Every now and again, he would switch on his bedside lamp and jot down a few notes. He was up and dressed by 6.30 am.

When he walked into Blundergutts' shed, Simon was already sitting there drinking a large mug of tea. He felt slightly annoyed. Blundergutts was HIS mate, not Simon's, yet although Simon hardly knew Blundergutts, he was already there drinking tea, as if he'd known him for years.

"I wish I was coming with you," sighed Blundergutts.

"But you are, aren't you?" said Reuben.

"As I've told your friend Simon, I'm a grown man. I wish I was your age again, but I suppose thirty pounds an hour is better than nothing."

"I'm sorry to see that you live in a shed Mr. Blunderbuss," said Simon.

"Blundergutts, not Blunderbuss!" snapped Blundergutts. "Anyway, have you seen the price of houses around here lately?" he continued. "And another thing, I'm just too big and old to be scrambling around assembly halls and trying to hide, especially in a blooming donkey suit."

"Come on, Blundergutts," interjected Reuben. "You've got to come with us, even if you just hang around watching. You've got an old head on old shoulders. We need a person like you to lead us."

"Yeah, of course!" snapped Blundergutts in a sarcastic tone. "It won't look that suspicious if they see a man in his forties just hanging around the assembly hall will it? Anyway, it should be an old head on young shoulders!"

"Whatever," said Reuben. "Please, Blundergutts. Just be in this with us, even if just for moral support."

"Oh, alright then," agreed Blundergutts. "Just this once, but I can hardly remember my way round the school, let alone be your leader."

"Look," said Reuben. "We all want to benefit from this machine so we all need to muck in together. When you want a fantastic new job later, we'll help you out and besides, as you keep reminding me, we're paying you!"

"I do need some work, even if it is only for a couple of hours. I'm so short of cash," muttered Blundergutts.

"Everything's gone wrong over the last few years. Crashing into Mr. and Mrs Hopkins' conservatory gave me a terrible shock. It gave them a terrible shock too. I suppose that's why they sacked me on the spot. And when I felled the oak tree the wrong way and it landed across the church the other Sunday, the vicar was very, very angry. It wasn't my fault."

"No of course not!" muttered Reuben. "It never is!"

"It was you was it?" said a shocked Simon. "I was in the church with my parents, It was a terrible shock. The vicar was just saying how thankful and blessed we all are for the gifts that come from above, when a blooming great dead oak tree came crashing through the roof. It was a wonder no one was killed. Anyway, why do you keep having terrible accidents, Gutts?"

"Blundergutts, not Gutts!" blasted Blundergutts.

"As I'm getting to know you a bit more, I thought I could call you Gutts for short."

"Well you can't!"

"I think we'd better get going," said Reuben, diplomatically changing the subject. "Let's see if we can get into the school without anyone noticing."

"I think we need another trial run first!" said Blundergutts.

"There's no time for that," said Reuben. "Everything will be alright," Reuben assured him. "And as you saw yesterday, you don't need to be very bright to work it. It's idiot proof so you should be absolutely fine.

82

That donkey suit is so advanced and it's got so many different functions on it. You used some of them yesterday! There's a bite mode, trot mode, run mode, it's even got headlights," enthused Reuben, hoping it would rub off on Blundergutts.

"Oh yes, that is realistic!" shouted Blundergutts. "Have you ever seen a donkey with headlights?"

"They're hidden behind two fur flaps, and they've got high and low beams."

"I just think that this whole thing is now becoming stupid," mumbled Blundergutts. "And if we're going to the school, we'd better hurry up about it, or loads of people will have arrived and we'll be seen."

# Chapter Eleven

## Mr. Pride's Big Day

Mr. Pride was preparing for his big day and, as usual, moaning at his wife. "Oi! Where's my best tie? I must look even BETTER than usual for the Chief Inspector's visit."

Today he had on his best silver suit. He stared at the mirror as he slowly fastened his pink, floral tie. He pushed a neatly folded handkerchief into the top pocket of his suit, then moved his head forward and slowly pressed his lips against his own reflection in the mirror. There was a loud sucking sound as his pursed lips pulled away from the glass, leaving a smudge. "It's time for me to go and be awarded my well deserved prize," he laughed, trotting down the stairs. He marched down the garden path with his wife tottering along behind him.

"Morning, how are you?" asked a neighbour, poking his head over the garden fence.

"Better than you," replied Mr Pride, without even turning to look at him. He climbed into the back of the car. "Off you go, dear!" he said, while his wife pushed the gear stick into first. "This is the big one," he muttered. "Nothing can possibly go wrong."

"Stop here, not right outside the school entrance, woman! You know this car is over three years old. Anyway, good luck, darling," he said, leaning right over the front seats and blowing a kiss at his own reflection in the rear view mirror. He then quickly climbed out of the car without shutting the door and, with his head held high, strolled off towards the school entrance. He hadn't felt this excited and pleased with himself for years!

Reuben pulled open a window he knew had a broken catch, and went round and opened the fire exit doors.

Their whispers echoed around the large assembly hall as they carried the crate in.

They heaved out the donkey suit, then Reuben and Simon quickly carried the empty crate back outside and hid it under a laurel bush.

"You two get in it now!" Reuben ordered. He quickly helped Blundergutts and Simon to clamber into the donkey suit.

"What's the point of us being in this?" grumbled Blundergutts, pushing his feet into the front legs "I'm sick of the whole idea now!"

"If we are seen, I'll jump on your back and you gallop out of here," whispered Reuben. "I'll steer you by pulling on your ears. The gallop button is the far switch on the left, down in the hoof somewhere, I think."

"You think?" gasped Blundergutts. "Anyway, if they think the donkey's stuffed and then it starts to move, it won't look right. I can't remember where any of the switches are now. And what about if it jams shut again?"

Reuben wasn't listening. He pressed the zip shut button and there was a loud whine, then clunk, as Blundergutts and Simon were shut inside. He pinned a large label on to the side of the donkey, which read: TO DUZZLEWICK SCHOOL FOR BEING SO SUPER. I WISH THIS PRIZE STUFFED DONKEY TO BE LEFT IN THE ASSEMBLY HALL TO CELEBRATE THE EVEN GREATER DAY IN THE LIFE OF THE GREAT HEADTEACHER MR. PRIDE. VERY MUCH LOVE FROM HER MAJESTY QUEEN ELIZABETH THE SECOND. PS. PRINCE PHILIP SAYS HULLO AND KEEP UP THE GREAT WORK!

"Now don't move, will you," said Reuben. "I've put a notice on you. You'll be accepted now, so you can stand there watching the fun."

"But!" mumbled Blundergutts.

"Trust me, I know what I'm doing!" Reuben reassured him.

Mr. Pride was in his office, briefing all the teachers. "As you are all aware," he began, "we have the Chief Education Officer visiting us today. He is undoubtedly going to present me with a top award which I just know I deserve."

"What time does he plan to arrive, sir?" asked Mr Horns.

"He'll be arriving in time for the morning assembly, and I want everything…EVERYTHING to go very smoothly. Is that clear?"

"Yes, Mr. Pride," murmured the teachers, feeling even more nervous and stressed than usual.

"Oh, one more thing, you good honourable sir," said Mr Horns, anxiously.

"Yes!"

"Reuben and Simon escaped from this great school the other day so they probably won't be in today. What shall I do, sir? I need advice on giving them maximum punishment."

"Leave it for now," huffed Mr. Pride. "I can't be bothered with them now. I saw Reuben yesterday off sick AGAIN. Thinking about it, I'd rather they were as far away from the school as possible today. We don't want them arriving late again and lowering the standard of my great school. I'll see that they are well and truly punished…don't you worry about that, let me deal with them, Horns. Especially Reuben – he's off sick whenever he feels like it! That aunt of his just writes anything he wants. Last week it said that he had Dutch elm disease! Mind you, sometimes I do think he's got a head full of sawdust."

"Do you want me to play the piano this morning?" asked Mrs. Grovalton. She was very overweight and wore dresses like curtains, which hung right to the floor. She wore thick-lensed glasses and she'd had her thin grey hair permed specially for the occasion, but it had gone wrong, and now looked like a doormat glued to her head.

"Do you want me to play the piano this morning, what?" snapped Mr. Pride.

"Er...great sir and respected head teacher," murmured Mrs Grovalton.

"Yes, of course you are to play the piano...and show more respect for me...Don't forget that you all love me. I'm the greatest head teacher that you've ever seen...I don't care what you think...That is what I am!"

"Yes, your greatness," they all chorused.


"I can't stand this, it's so hot and uncomfortable," Blundergutts mumbled, as he grew hotter by the minute inside the donkey suit.

"I can't see anything!" complained Simon.

"So what?" replied Reuben. "As long as your body holds up the back half of the donkey... Anyway, I've got to sort out this pile of boxes to hide behind."

"I can now see out of the eyes, but it's agony just standing here in a bent hunched position," groaned Blundergutts. "My back is killing me! I want compensation for this!"

"Shoosh! Be quiet!" said Reuben "I can hear someone coming." He clambered behind the piano and pulled the Mind Machine from the case and slid it out of the padded sack. He switched it on just to make sure it had power. Dials flickered and burst into life.

Mr. Mopping, the caretaker, was shocked to see a rigid donkey standing in the assembly hall. "What the blazes!" he gasped, walking over to it and peering at the notice. "A present from 'er Majesty the Queen.Ol' Pride will like that," he spluttered through his gums. He then walked off to Mr. Pride's office. He banged on the door and walked in. "Somefink impor'ant... very impor'ant 'as just arrived at the school, sir," he announced with an air of importance.

"It's me of course...why tell me about me? What are you thinking about man?" retorted Mr. Pride.

"No! No!"

"What!" shouted Mr. Pride, rising to his feet. "If you don't believe that I am great, not only are you wrong, but you can walk away from this school right now, NEVER EVER TO COME BACK!!. CARETAKERS ARE TWO A PENNY!"

"No... you don't un'erstand...you 'ave a present from 'er Majesty the Queen! And there's also a message from Prince Philip saying 'keep up the good work.'"

"What? Where is it then man?" demanded Mr. Pride, impatiently. "Why didn't you say it was from the Queen?"

"I just 'ave. It's a stuffed donkey, and it's in the assembly 'all."

"What? Let me take a look."

They both hurried into the hall.

"You're right…A present from the Queen…But a stuffed donkey?" gasped Mr Pride. "How did it get here?"

"I dunno, sir."

"You don't know much, do you?" grumbled Mr. Pride. "Maybe that's why you're only a caretaker. Very well, leave it there. At least this will be a tremendous boost to my ego and image, and one more thing on show for the Inspector. "

Blundergutts and Simon remained in their still rigid positions. Simon felt his heart pounding through his head when he heard the voices so close to him, particularly the voice of Mr. Pride.

Reuben remained in a crouched position behind the piano.

Half an hour later the hall was packed. Children sat in their seats and kept staring at the donkey.

"Stop moving!" Blundergutts kept huffing in a muffled voice.

"Alright! I'm trying!" grunted Simon. "But I'm so uncomfortable…Can't I sit down?"

"No!" mumbled Blundergutts. "A stuffed animal usually stays in one position. It will look suspicious if half the donkey suddenly sits down, you idiot! Do you not think that I'm uncomfortable as well? My knees are killing me!"

There was a rumble of chairs as all the children stood up. A line of dreary-looking teachers stepped on to the stage and took their seats. Just the very sight of Mr. Horns gave Reuben the creeps.

Mrs. Grovalton sat down heavily on to the piano stool, which creaked as she wriggled her bottom to get comfortable.

Reuben felt terrified. "Why did I take this on?" he thought. "It's just too much. Why did I have to suggest using the donkey suit? What a fool I've been!" Everything seemed so complicated and real to Reuben now.

Mr. Pride strode into the hall. His shoes echoed loudly as he walked up the steps and on to the stage. Everyone in the hall fell silent.

"Good morning children!" he said in a loud commanding voice. "Who's the greatest headteacher in the land?"

"You are, sir!" they all forcefully chorused.

"Jolly good," said Mr Pride. He pulled out a small mirror from his pocket and winked at his own reflection, then swiftly pushed it back into his pocket.

A bent over elderly man slowly walked into the hall. He had small round glasses and a wisp of grey hair trying to cover his bald patch. His large nose was very red and reminded Reuben of an elongated strawberry. He had two large teeth protruding out over his bottom lip.

"Ah!" shouted Mr. Pride. "Children! This is Mr. Crabbs, the chief and most senior School Inspector in the county. He has come here today to allow us to prove, yet again, what a great school Duzzlewick is. When he has seen this for himself he will almost undoubtedly be presenting me with a top award for the best school in West Sussex, and, I might now add…this donkey here is a personal gift to me, from Her Majesty the Queen, showing her appreciation for all my work, and Prince Philip absolutely LOVES me!"

Mr. Crabbs staggered up on to the stage. His saggy cheeks wobbled as he sat down on to the waiting chair. His eyes widened slightly as a sound of passing wind came from the donkey.

"I can hardly breath!" mumbled Simon.

"We will commence with a hymn," continued Mr. Pride. "Hymn number sixty-one. 'Oh ye of little faith come unto me'. Hymn number sixty-one."

The piano burst into life, nearly deafening Reuben.

After the hymn was sung, Mr. Pride remained standing. He puffed out his chest and gave a loud cough. "Welcome to another assembly. Mr. Horns is going to read some excellent poetry all about me and my school… Mr. Horns please."

Mr. Horns rose nervously to his feet.

Mr. Pride sat down and folded his arms, waiting for these poems, which would show just how great he is.

"He's wearing the same jacket that he wore when he taught me, except that it's now got holes under the armpits," came a muffled voice from the front of the donkey.

"AAAAGH!" screamed Mrs. Grovalton.

"What's the matter with you, my dear?" said Mr. Pride, being extra polite and trying to contain his anger in front of the Inspector.

"I heard the donkey speak!"

"Put less gin with your cornflakes, Mrs. Grovalton," said Mr. Pride, unable to remain pleasant for more than a few seconds.

Mr. Crabbs looked up and stared at Mrs. Grovalton and then at the 'stuffed' donkey.

"Right Mr. Horns, continue please," said Mr. Pride.

"Is that tatty old donkey really a present from the Queen?" whispered Mr. Crabbs to Mr Gibbons, the P.E teacher, who was completely bald and weighed over twenty-five stone, but all the children loved him as he was so easy going and kind.

"I suppose it must be if Mr. Pride said it is," wheezed Mr. Gibbons. "It apparently arrived this morning, but no one actually knows how it got in here. The caretaker just noticed it this morning, with a note on it with a message from the Queen, or so it says."

"Oh," said Mr. Crabbs, raising his eyebrows. "Hang on a minute! It might be a huge bomb, about to go off at any moment."

"What, from the Queen?" remarked a startled Mr Gibbons.

"No, no, I mean from someone pretending it's from the Queen!" Mr. Crabbs explained.

"What's all the mumbling about?" snapped Mr Pride. "I didn't mean you of course sir, Mr. Crabbs, ha, ha, ha!"

"There might be a bomb inside that donkey," said Mr. Gibbons.

"I haven't time to look now," snapped Mr. Pride. "Besides, I do not respect anything you say, you're only a P.E. Teacher."

Mr. Crabbs slightly opened his mouth with disbelief at overhearing Mr. Pride's comment to Mr. Gibbons.

"Come on Horns, get on with the poem!" said Mr. Pride impatiently.

Mr. Horns cleared his throat and stared at the piece of paper.

"Oh great Mr. Pride,

"I love having you by my side,"

he said with a quivering, dramatic voice.

Reuben started typing a poem as quickly and quietly as possible into the Mind Machine. His fingers quivered with nerves as he pressed the action button.

"You, oh great you," Mr. Horns continued. Then his face suddenly went pale and his mouth dropped open.

"Oh Mr. dog's breath Pride,

like warm cow-pats you do glide."

"Oi! Stop this insulting rubbish about great me!" shouted Mr. Pride rising to his feet.

A little earlier, Reuben had inadvertently hit a small switch with his elbow, switching on the the voice activating dictionary. The woman's voice from the machine piped up. "GOOD MORNING!" she announced, her loud piercing voice echoing around the hall. "A COW-PAT IS A FLAT ROUND PIECE OF COW-DUNG. GLIDE MEANS: MOVE WITH A SMOOTH CONTINUOUS MOTION. THANK YOU FOR YOUR TIME!"

Reuben just managed to find the switch and mute the voice.

"Who's that butting in and stating the obvious?" shouted Mr. Pride, looking around the hall. "And you can stop your useless, vile poems at once, Horns! Unless they're about someone else!"

Mr. Crabbs was now sitting bolt upright on the edge of his seat, his mouth wide open as he stared in shock at Mr. Pride and Mr. Horns.

"May I continue, slurry-face Pride?" asked Mr. Horns.

"I got that one in, quick," thought Reuben.

"Will whoever it is, stop using a typewriter!" shouted Mr. Pride. "And no you can't continue Horns. In fact I want you sacked."

The pupils sat in a shocked silence, wondering what might happen next.

Mr. Crabbs was now sitting RIGHT on the edge of his seat, writing furiously into his notebook.

Simon could stand the strain no longer. His legs collapsed, dragging Blundergutts down too, and the donkey buckled up and crashed to the floor.

"AAAAAAAGH!" screamed Mrs. Grovalton.

"Obviously poor quality!" said Mr Pride. "I'm surprised at the Queen. If you can't rely on the Queen who on earth can you rely on? Still, she's not as well off as she used to be. It's probably come from a charity shop. John Johnson...you're big and strong, remove that cheap stuffed donkey at once!"

John Johnson walked over to the donkey and grabbed its tail. Blundergutts' hand accidentally pushed the kick button. A hind leg sprung out and the hoof smacked Johnson square on the nose. Without saying a word, he crashed into the front row. A loud gasp of surprise burst from the pupils.

"Good Lord!" shouted Mr. Crabbs.

"AAAAAAGH!" screamed Mrs. Grovalton.

Blundergutts' hand accidentally pushed a kick button again. A hind leg flew out and struck the piano causing a terrific clang, which reverberated around the hall.

Mrs. Grovalton clambered off the stool. "The donkey's alive!" she screamed.

Both rear legs of the donkey suddenly kicked out

with a huge whoosh and the hooves slammed straight into her chest.

"AAAAAAARRRGH!!" she yelled in absolute agony, crashing to the floor, clasping her hands to her chest, her mouth wide open, and her head shaking from side to side.

Suddenly, Blundergutts' sweaty hands slipped again and pushed both kick buttons and the whole donkey leaped in the air and kicked out, with both back legs, before crashing to the floor, landing right on top of Mrs. Grovalton. "OOOOOoooooofff!" she wheezed.

"Ring the Teaching Agency for a replacement!" ordered Mr. Pride, to a shocked-looking secretary on the end of the row. "By the look of things, Grovalton will be off for weeks and we'll be short staffed."

With its stiff grey legs waving in the air, the donkey rolled off Mrs. Grovalton.

She slowly crawled over to the stage, her fatty arms shook and quivered as she painfully hauled herself to her feet. She then just stood there staring at the floor and gasping for air, while holding her chest with one hand and the edge of the stage with the other.

Blundergutts and Simon felt hot and confused as the donkey rolled over several times along the floor, then it half stood up, its face looking twisted and glazed as its head wobbled.

"Good gracious!" shouted Mr. Crabbs. "It can't possibly be alive, surely. The stuffing company should be reprimanded! This is preposterous!"

Blundergutts' hand accidentally knocked against a button half way up the donkey's leg. There was a loud bang from the donkey's rear end followed by a loud slap. Mr. Crabbs rose to his feet. His face was completely covered in a round, stiff, brown, soggy mass. "UUUUGh! he gasped, raising his hands in the air."

There was a loud gasp of shock followed by stifled giggling from the pupils.

The big thick home made donkey pat slithered down Mr. Crabbs's face and dropped on to Mr. Gibbon's head, making him now look as if he had a full head of thick shiny brown hair.

"What's this on my head?" gasped Mr. Gibbons, wheezing as he rose to his feet, and feeling the gooey mass with his fat fingers.

Mr. Crabbs staggered down the steps to get a closer look at the donkey.

"Let's get out of here!" shouted Reuben.

Blundergutts scurried forward, and Simon had to follow. Blundergutts was desperately trying to line up his eyes with the eye holes in the donkey's face. He crashed into Mr. Crabbs and at the same time, accidentally pushed the Bite Button. The donkey's big square teeth ripped into Mr. Crabbs's arm. There was then a terrific ripping sound as his whole suit sleeve, followed by his shirtsleeve, were torn off. "AAARGH!" he bellowed, showing a set of very brown sticky-looking teeth. He then spat some more lumps of 'fake' dung from his mouth.

"I just can't believe what I'm seeing!" wailed Mr. Pride. "I'll sort out this wild animal...how dare he bite the great man who is going to give me an award! I thought it was stuffed!"

"How dare you! I am not stuffed!" bellowed Mr. Crabbs, still rubbing his bare arm.

"No, not you, great sir...the donkey."

"Well get your grammar right then!" shouted Mr. Crabbs. "You linked me grammatically to the stuffed donkey."

But Mr. Pride wasn't listening as he picked up a large broom and charged forward. He swished the broom down again and again on the donkey's hindquarters, but there was just a loud dull thump as it bounced off the chain-mail strengthened fur. There was suddenly a wave of suppressed laughter from the pupils. Blundergutts's tired arms slid down into the hoofs, hitting every button as they went, including the machine-gun-dung-switch. The donkey's mouth snapped wide open giving a loud EEEAAAAW! Then both back legs kicked up again and banged Mr. Pride in the chest. "OOOOF!!" he gasped. Then his head jerked back five times as five brown lumps smacked him in the face one after the other. He mumbled a few words as he crashed to the floor.

A roar of louder laughter erupted from the spectating pupils.

"Silence!" shouted Mr. Pride, clambering to his feet. Pulling his handkerchief from his top pocket, he rubbed it around his brown face and neck. "This is a not a pantomime, this is a very serious school assembly. It's NOT funny!" he bellowed.

"Get your legs in sync so we can run!" bellowed Blundergutts.

The donkey's hooves squeaked and skidded as it tried to pick up speed along the wood floor. The children turned their heads as they watched aghast, their mouths wide open.

"Grab it, someone!" bellowed Mr Pride. But everyone just sat there motionless, in shocked disbelief, and trying not to laugh.

Reuben leapt up from behind the piano and grabbed the donkey by both ears. It staggered and skidded about behind him as he pulled with all his might and guided it across the hall and round to the main entrance. The double doors swung wildly as he barged through them and ran up the corridor.

"Out this way!" he shouted, leading the donkey out of the school.

"Stand here for a minute while I go back and get the machine. I nearly forgot it!"

"Hurry up then!" shouted Bert.

Reuben ran back into the noise and chaos. He managed to surreptitiously pick up the machine, stuff it back in to its case, and rush back out, without being noticed.

Holding the case with one hand, the donkey's mane with the other, he guided the staggering donkey across the playing field. When they reached a clump of trees, Reuben hit the unzip button. There was a pause, then a whirring sound and Blundergutts and Simon fell out and lay on the ground, trying to catch their breath.

"Never again! I thought the zip wasn't going to open!" puffed Blundergutts wiping sweat from his face. "I've only clocked up one hour fifty five minutes," he said, looking at his watch.

"We'll pay you for two hours then," Reuben reassured him.

"This has been an absolutely horrific experience!" grumbled Simon, flicking sweat off his face with his finger-tips.

"You always were a bit of a moaner," Reuben smirked.

## Back at the school

"I think you had better just give me the award, King Crabbs," said Mr. Pride, still trying to wipe fake dung from the corners of his eyes and mouth.

"Oh no, no, no, no! You are going to be suspended as of now," Mr. Crabbs replied emphatically, still rubbing his bare severely bruised arm. "And stop calling me King Crabbs! This is a school you are supposed to be running! The only person deserving a reward, is that boy who dragged the donkey out whether it was real, stuffed, or what, I don't care. What a fine lad, putting the reputation of the school before his own safety! If everyone was like him, whoever he was, this school and the world, I'm sure, would be a much better place. He's the only one who deserves a reward. But you? You are an utter disgrace to the teaching profession and totally incompetent. How could you have allowed all this to happen? I shall recommend that you never ever, ever, ever, run a school again!"

The next day Reuben, Simon and Blundergutts gathered for a meeting at Blundergutts' Shed.

"Wow! What a day we had yesterday," grinned Reuben, raising his mug of tea, "I think we should drink to the rest of our successful lives."

"Well I don't think it was that good, in fact it was terrible for Simon and me," moaned Blundergutts. "I just did not see the point in the whole thing."

"You haven't read the local paper, have you," said Reuben. He thumbed his way through and found the right page. "Headteacher of Duzzlewick School resigns." he read aloud. "And Reuben Oxley, 14, has been recommended for a medal for being a very brave pupil with high morals and exemplary self-sacrificing behaviour."

"Wow! Do you deserve it, ha,ha?" mocked Blundergutts. "And I wonder who the new headteacher is going to be? He might be worse than Mr. Pride."

"I doubt it," said Reuben. "Because with the help of the machine, the new headteacher will be YOU!"

"I fancy a big important job – it's my dream!" said Blundergutts.

"Let's have a toast," said Reuben, raising his mug. "To our new headteacher!"

"And to the Amazing Mind Machine!" added Simon.

The clatter of three mugs knocking together and their roars of laughter drowned out the sound of a furious Gramps' pale knuckles, knocking on the shed door.

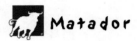

For exclusive discounts on Matador titles,
sign up to our occasional newsletter at
troubador.co.uk/bookshop